JOEL MANNERS

THE ARTIFICER'S TALE

A TALE FROM

THE MARTYR'S WORLD

The Artificer's Tale

By Joel Manners

This is a work of fiction. Names, characters, places, and incidents either are the product of the author's imagination or are used fictitiously. Any resemblance to actual persons, living or dead, events, or locales is entirely coincidental.

Copyright © 2017 Joel Manners

All rights reserved. This book or any portion thereof may not be reproduced or used in any manner whatsoever without the express written permission of the author except for the use of brief quotations in a book review or scholarly journal.

This book is available in print and electronic format at most online retailers.

Cover art and map by Joel Manners

ISBN 978-0-9972594-6-9

Colqhoun Books
2407 Pruett St.
Austin, TX. 78703

www.JoelManners.com

Books by Joel Manners

THE CHRONICLES OF THE MARTYR

THE MARTYR'S BLADE

THE MARTYR'S TEARS

TALES FROM THE MARTYR'S WORLD

THE ARTIFICER'S TALE

THE THIEF'S TALE (*announced*)

For all the meddling kids out there.

Table of Contents

THE ARTIFICER'S TALE

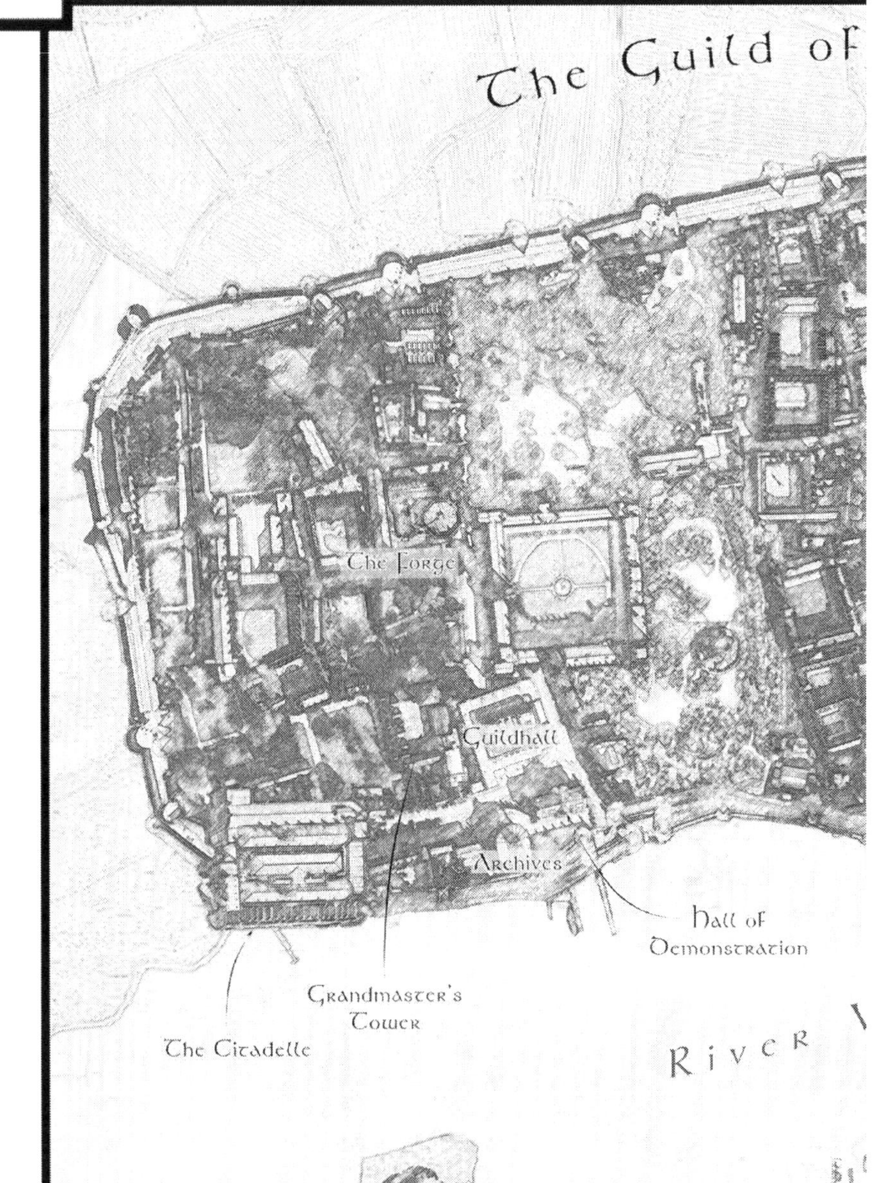
The Guild of
The Forge
Guildhall
Archives
Hall of
Demonstration
Grandmaster's
Tower
The Citadelle
River
The Docks

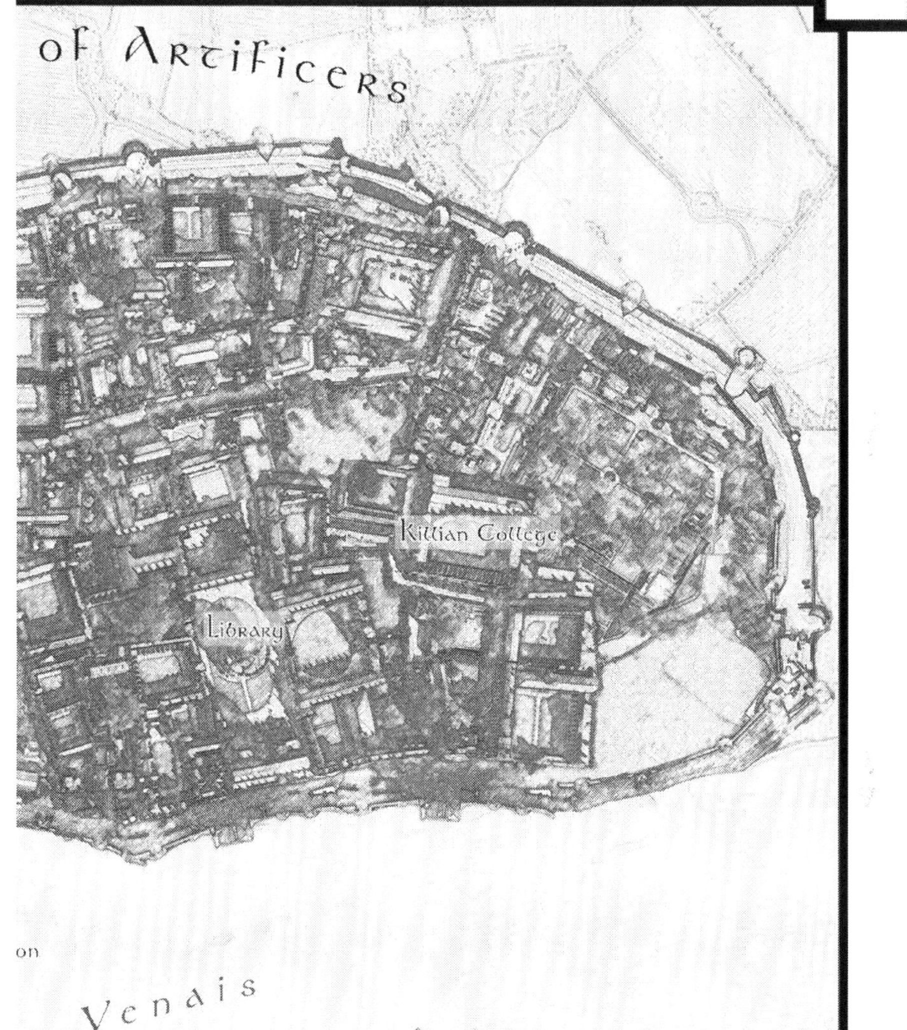

of Artificers
Killian College
Library
on
R Venais
ks
Criénne

Rikard

"Do you see here, how Master Lorcan has created a second declension of strength and juxtaposed it against an influence of descending tones? Do you see the interaction?" Master Quentin's voice echoed amongst the soaring pillars and empty benches of the ancient room. "The beauty of the structure lies in the alignment of offsetting concepts, each within its own house, yet that is not Master Lorcan's true genius. Can anyone tell us what that would be?"

Quentin paused, and his gaze moved expectantly over the four apprentices who stood timidly on the opposite side of the table. All four stared rigidly at the Device that lay on the table, reverently spread open to reveal its inner structure. The Device itself was a creation of beauty, twin spirals of delicate metal that embraced a series of cunningly wrought flanges that opened and closed like the petals of a flower, revealing a heart of onyx inlaid with runes and patterns of silver.

Quentin let the silence weigh heavily on his apprentices, and Rikard caught Dominique's glance from the corner of his eye. She tilted her head toward Quentin, urging Rikard to speak, but he could only give her a rueful grin in return. He had no idea what

Grandmaster Lorcan's true genius might be, or where it might be hidden in the exquisite metal creation that lay on the table in front of him.

The hall was silent, save for the distant, cascading tones of Polonius' Chronometer signaling noon and the quiet rumble of an apprentice's stomach in response. Ornate wooden benches rose in tiers on all sides of them, worn from centuries of use, their red cushions the only color amongst the dark wood and grey stone of the soaring walls. A wooden balcony supported a second bank of benches behind a carved rail, and elegant pillars lined the circumference, supporting the distant arc of the paneled ceiling, from which hung dozens of chandeliers on long chains.

Rikard looked forward to the times when Quentin decided to teach in the Hall of Demonstration. Its elegant grandeur stood in testament to the ancient power of the Guild's craft, and the rows of benches to the inheritance of the thousands of masters who had honed their skills on this very floor. A tall painting in the Commons showed the Hall of Demonstration packed with artificers, their faces filled with wonder as Grandmaster Hubert empowered a shining star. The hall was unchanged from the time of the painting, though Hubert had led the Guild a century before the Cataclysm. Only the cushions were different. They had favored green in Hubert's day. Rikard stood now upon the exact spot that Hubert occupied on that long-ago day, and Rikard could practically hear the murmur of excitement that must have rolled through the crowd.

But Rikard had never seen the hall used for lecturing, nor for the demonstration of craft for which it was named. It stood empty, save for the occasional small lesson such as Quentin conducted today, and the days upon which an apprentice was elevated to master. Only then did the masters gather in their formal robes to watch their new brethren initiated. Only then did the hall regain the grandeur of Hubert's time.

The apprentices were beginning to fidget uncomfortably, and Rikard spent a moment loosening the elegant drape of his white robes, for the hall was beginning to grow warm as the sun reached its zenith, the coolness of the morning slipping away between the stone archways. The spring sun had none of the intensity it would gain in just a few months, but Criénne lacked the cool sea breezes of Rikard's home in Vordoux.

Dominique gave Rikard another discrete glance, urging him to reply. Quentin appeared content to let his apprentices perish from hunger before answering his own question, but Rikard was not sure why the burden of looking a fool should fall to him. *More a fool,* he decided, as standing and staring at his sandaled feet could not look especially wise. In any case, he knew he would be the first to answer. Rikard trusted in his ability to make any nonsense sound reasonable, and he was fairly certain he could get past Quentin's scrutiny if he stayed as general as possible. *Besides, a chance to earn some favor from Dominique should not be squandered,* he reasoned. Rikard allowed himself another glance at the girl with the fair hair of the north and the dark skin of the Summer Coast. As far as he knew, Dominique had spent the entire year since they had been made apprentice artificers doing nothing but studying, but if she were to ever allow herself to glance around at the adoring stares of her fellow apprentices, Rikard wanted to make sure that his gaze was the one that she returned.

"Resonance, Master Quentin?" Rikard ventured, brushing a flop of thick, black hair out of his eyes.

"Well-guessed, Rikard. But what of resonance? There are other, easier ways to create resonance, are there not? Apparently, I am mistaken, judging from your blank stares."

"I'm sorry, Master Quentin. I'm not sure I even understand what Master Lorcan's structure would do." Rikard smiled apologetically. *Oh, well, it was a good guess.* "Would it not simply cause a lesser contrast? And how would the adept access it? There's nothing in the Word at all."

"But it does. You can see that it does."

"Yes, Master Quentin, I'm sorry."

"Don't be," Quentin assured his student, and he indicated the Device on the table in front of them with a sweep of his hand. "Grandmaster Lorcan's work is seminal. Few understand what it does, let alone how it does it. But *that* is today's lesson. You are not builders, nor blacksmiths. Devices are not the products of the recipes of iron and charcoal, nor of load and support, with only one intent and only one result. You will paint with the Maker's brush, and your art touches creation itself."

"Yes, Master Quentin," Dominique ventured, "but how does Grandmaster Lorcan's structure work?"

"Of course, Dominique. How, indeed. Here, examine the interaction between the structures. Lorcan realized that as they were empowered this layer of the declension would naturally be energized, resting as it does at the foci, and that it would, therefore, be in harmony with—do you find this terribly tedious, Apprentice Rikard?"

"No, Master Quentin, it's just, look." Rikard pointed over Quentin's shoulder, and the master glanced to follow the apprentice's finger toward the back wall of the hall.

There stood a tall alcove, designed from the time of the hall's construction to house a single Device, a globe of crystal that hung suspended between thin columns of gold which were crafted to resemble interlocking strands of honeysuckle. The globe was filled with a glowing mist that sent forth a gentle light that ebbed and grew as the mist slowly swirled to the pressure of some unfelt breeze. Rikard had examined the Device many times, fascinated by its inexplicable longevity as much as by the cunning way the globe was contained by the vines. The Device was present in Hubert's painting, no different in paint than it had appeared every day Rikard had seen it in the hall.

However, the Device was changing now. Silver light swirled into the globe, spreading in twists and eddies until it filled the crystal with a radiance so brilliant the artificers were forced to shade their eyes and turn away. A ringing chime sounded through the hall, clear and keen, and it throbbed in Rikard's ears as if a silver fork had been struck against a stone.

"Dominique, fetch Grandmaster Dorian, or any of the grandmasters, whomever you can find. Hurry." Quentin began to reassemble Lorcan's Device, his fingers deft and sure as he secured the delicate instrument. Once the shell was back in place he lowered the Device into its case, fastened the latch, and handed the mahogany box to Rikard. "Return this to the archives. The rest of you, out."

Rikard held the box carefully against his chest, but he paused in the doorway, his gaze drawn to the glowing Device at the end of the Hall. Its chime sang through him, at times strong enough that he felt his jaw ache in response, at times so faint that it felt merely a whisper. The crystal sent bright rays of light dancing through the room, casting rainbows of color across the wood panels and stone pillars. Rikard watched until his eyes were dazzled and he turned away, his vision ruined by dark spots that danced and leapt before his gaze.

"Quentin, what on earth…"

Rikard could not see who spoke from the entrance to the hall, but he did not need to. The rich baritone was unmistakable.

"Grandmaster Dorian," Quentin replied, "thank you for coming so quickly."

"I did not believe young Dominique, but she was quite insistent. Is this your doing?"

"No, Grandmaster. I was teaching Lorcan's Star when the globe empowered itself."

"Nonsense." Dorian's face gradually emerged from the spots that darkened Rikard's gaze, the flowing white beard and craggy, aquiline nose of the grandmaster becoming clearer with every moment. Dorian smoothed his beard against his chin as he watched the play of light within the globe, his wiry brows creased in thought. "Devices do not empower themselves. If no new Word was used, then this is merely the result of its original Word."

"There was no new Word," Quentin assured the grandmaster. "I felt nothing."

"Then it has finally…" Dorian said softly before turning a sharp gaze onto Rikard. "Who was here to see it? Besides Rikard and yourself?"

"Only my apprentices."

"All of them?"

"Yes, Grandmaster."

Grandmaster Dorian nodded, his gaze hooded, and then turned his back on the apprentice. Quentin made shooing motions with his hands until Rikard reluctantly left the room, closing the massive wooden doors behind him.

A crowd of apprentices had gathered outside the Hall of Demonstration, drawn by the resonant song of the Device within. They clustered amongst the tall pillars that supported the atrium's balconies and lined the stone railings of the stairs that ascended along the wall of the normally quiet room. But now its stone walls echoed with the growing swell of dozens of conversations and shouted questions, despite the masters' best efforts to drive the crowd away with waving arms and stern scowls.

Rikard stuck to the wall and quickly slipped down the small hallway that led to the Close, leaving the hubbub behind. His sandals slapped echoes from the marble floor as he hurried, his long stride causing his robes to billow around his legs and shoulders as he moved.

A figure waited for him at the doors to the Close, her white apprentice robes a brilliant contrast to her dark skin.

"What did he say?" Dominique asked as soon as Rikard drew near, her dark eyes sparkling with excitement. "Dorian told me to go back to college, but I couldn't before I found out what was going on."

"Walk with me to the archives." Rikard patted the polished wooden lid of the box. "I need to put this back before someone realizes they gave Lorcan's Star to an apprentice to carry around with him."

The midday sun shone unabated into the Close, baking the red marble of the floor and walls, so the apprentices walked along the edge, keeping to the cool shadows behind the tall pillars that lined the long courtyard. On either side, ancient stone walls rose three stories high, with tall, thin windows framed between the pillars and the high arches that capped them. Fountains bubbled and splashed along the center, casting small, dark stains across the red marble that quickly dried in the warm sun. At the far end of the Close, the entrance to the archives loomed, a wide dais flanked by taller pillars, and a sheer face of marble, unblemished by windows that might allow a careless gaze to witness any of the secrets kept within.

And beyond the archive, the soaring tower of the Forge thrust into the bold blue of the cloudless sky. Rank after rank of engraved arches stacked one upon the other until it was easy to lose count of how many there were, and within the arches, the featureless black stone of the Forge itself.

"What happened after I left?" Dominique asked again, impatience pushing a small wrinkle between her faint eyebrows.

"It kept chiming, sometimes loud, sometimes soft, but it never stopped. It never stopped glowing either." Rikard considered what he had seen more diligently. "And Grandmaster Dorian seemed extremely excited, although he tried to pretend like there was nothing strange going on. I don't think he liked that we were there."

"No," Dominique agreed. "Dorian was very excited when I told him which Device it was. He almost skipped the whole way there. But when we arrived at the hall, he told me off, as if it was my fault I was there."

Rikard nodded and contented himself with watching his companion as they walked. Dominique was shorter than he but had long legs and a slim figure that made her appear taller than she was. She had braided her blonde hair into a long tail that swayed back and forth across the small of her back, and the light cloth of her short robes pulled against her in interesting ways as she walked, much to Rikard's delight. She wore open sandals, with thin leather ties that wound around her smooth calves until they disappeared under the hem of her robe. Rikard felt a smile grow uncontrollably across his face, and he decided that he had been assigned worse errands to run.

"It is called Aldric's Gaze," Dominique murmured to herself, puzzling Rikard as he tried to connect her words with what he had been gazing at. He must have frowned, for she graced Rikard with an apologetic smile. "The Device, I mean. The globe. I read about it in the library."

"For Grandmaster Aldric?" Rikard asked, searching his memory for the small traces that remained of the history he had forced into his brain during the first weeks of his apprenticeship. "He was one of the founders, wasn't he? Do you think it's one of his?"

"Yes, he was a founder. The first Grandmaster, and I would guess it was one of his Devices. It must be, to be displayed in the Hall, don't you think? It didn't say what it was looking for, though. Aldric's Gaze," she explained. "It just said that was its name."

"But, wasn't he hundreds and hundreds of years ago? Before the Cataclysm?"

"One thousand years ago," Dominique agreed.

"Can you imagine, a Device that still worked from being empowered one thousand years ago."

"If it was his, and if he empowered it. People name things all sorts of stupid names."

"True," Rikard laughed, and the sound bounced happily off the stone walls around them.

They reached the archives, and Dominique stopped at the foot of the stairs, staring at the edifice with her hands on her hips and a frown of concentration on her face. Rikard left her to her thoughts for a moment, then apologetically cleared his throat. "I need to take this in." Rikard gestured toward the archives with the mahogany box.

Dominique frowned at him, then her face cleared and she smiled. "While you are in there, see if you can ask someone about Aldric. I'll see you back at college."

Then she turned away and hurried from the Close, leaving behind the faint scent of rosemary soap, and Rikard breathed a deep sigh of contentment. He ascended the dozen steps, pushed open the heavy, wooden doors at their top, and entered the cool darkness of the archives.

It took Rikard far longer to complete his errand than he could ever have imagined. He had not wanted to leave the Star with the porter who manned the doors, and so he was forced to wait in the echoing foyer while the porter found a master and convinced him to come to the doors with him. And then, of course, Rikard had to explain how it was that he came to be in possession of one of the Guild's greatest treasures when clearly he could not have legitimately secured the artifact from the archives in the first place.

When at last Rikard emerged, blinking, into the Close, the shadows from the western wall lay almost completely across the ground, within a hand's-breadth of touching the base of the line of pillars against the opposite wall. Rikard's stomach suddenly twisted with hunger as he realized how late it was, and he lengthened his stride, hoping to catch the cooks before they began preparing for dinner.

He had barely reached the bottom of the archive steps, however, when he was brought up short by a call from across the Close.

"Apprentice Rikard?" A master who Rikard did not recognize strode toward him from the direction of the Grandmaster's Tower, his raised hand gesturing impatiently for Rikard to join him. "You are Rikard?"

"Yes, Master," Rikard nodded.

"Grandmaster Dorian is waiting for you," the master said accusingly. "In his study. Right away, please."

What have I done? Rikard pushed his hair into place, smoothed his robe and followed the master through the wide doors of the Grandmaster's Tower. Their footsteps echoed in the vast silence of soaring pillars and wide marble spaces as they passed through empty halls and along endless passageways. Long shafts of golden light lancing through the air from high windows blazed against the cool stone, and Rikard's robes flashed and faded with every stride.

Grandmaster Dorian's chambers spread along a wide terrace overlooking the Garden Palace . Rikard was ushered into the study through tall doors made of black wood studded in silver, and they closed behind the apprentice with a soft thud as his guide beat a hasty retreat.

Rikard hesitated, unsure of his bearings. Bright light poured into the study through an archway that led to the terrace at the far end of the room, blinding as it reflected from the polished marble of the walls and floor. Rikard's shoulders hunched involuntarily as he tentatively crossed the featureless floor toward the glare, his gaze flickering vainly around the room in search of any guide to indicate what was expected of him.

"Apprentice Rikard, where have you been?" a voice called out to him, echoing from the cold stone walls.

"At the… at the archives, Grandmaster Dorian," Rikard stammered, unsure of which direction to address. "Master Quentin asked me to return Lorcan's Star, Grandmaster."

Rikard hurried forward a dozen steps and stopped abruptly. A massive desk of black stone sprawled across the middle of the room, dwarfing the cluster of elegant wooden chairs in front of it. Rikard squinted against the light from the terrace and realized that he was not alone.

Grandmaster Dorian stood in the center of the archway with his hands clasped behind his back, his white hair a glowing mane against the light. Master Quentin stood next to the grandmaster, a frown of stern disapproval sending deep furrows across his brow, while Dominique, Clément, and Theirn were seated in the ancient chairs in front of the desk. None of his fellow apprentices greeted him with more than a quick glance and wide, worried eyes.

"It took you this long to return a Device to the archives?" Quentin's eyebrows arched in bristling surprise.

"Yes, sir, there was some confusion."

Quentin nodded and indicated the last chair in front of the desk. "Sit down, Rikard, you have taken up enough of the grandmaster's time already."

Rikard hurried to do as he was told, perching on the hard, wooden chair with the grandmaster looming uncomfortably above him.

"Now that you are all here," Grandmaster Dorian began, somehow infusing his voice with a reproach that made Rikard squirm with shame, "I must speak with you about what you saw today. None of you have achieved your master's robes, yet the oath you swore to defend the mysteries of the Guild when you became apprentices is no less binding. Today you have seen one of those mysteries, and it is for this very reason that all apprentices take that oath. Do you understand?"

"Yes, Grandmaster," Rikard mumbled along with the other three apprentices.

"To reveal what you have seen will brand you as an apostate," Grandmaster Dorian spat the word with contempt, "and you will suffer the grim fate of all who choose that path." Dorian paced slowly across the room to the far wall, where two small, glowing Diviners held by stone ravens guarded a closed door, letting the silence weigh on the apprentices as he watched them with a sharp gaze.

Rikard kept his face lowered, his eyes riveted on the shining reflection on the surface of the table. *Apostate?* Rikard knew the punishment for betraying the Guild, and had known for years before he became an apprentice, as did any boy who loved legends of dark mystery and horrific death. The fact that dire warnings as to the consequences of betraying the Guild had featured prominently in every stage of becoming an apprentice had only enhanced Rikard's grim fascination with the dark tales. *But we haven't betrayed the Guild… we just saw a Device!*

Rikard could not help risking a glance at his fellow apprentices. Clément's gaze was focused unwaveringly on a spot on the floor just in front of his feet, while Theirn had apparently decided that locking his stare on the grandmaster was the best way to avoid reprimand, although judging from the apprentice's ashen skin he was regretting that decision.

Dominique met Rikard's gaze and quickly glanced to the desk and back with a slight nod of her head. Rikard examined the desk as well as he could without risking raising his head. The desk's wide, black surface was nearly as bare as the rest of the room, but several orderly stacks of books rested near the grandmaster's ornate chair. One of the books lay open on the desk, ready for the chair's occupant to review. The book was remarkable, with silver bindings and a thick case with elegant hinges and prominent locks, but Rikard's eye was caught by what was on the open pages. The yellowed vellum was covered in tiny writing in black ink, unreadable at Rikard's distance, surrounding a beautiful drawing of a Device. Its shell was removed in the drawing, but even so, Rikard recognized Aldric's Gaze.

"Do not speak to anyone of what you witnessed," Dorian waited for each apprentice to meet his eye and nod acceptance. "Very well. You are dismissed."

The apprentices gratefully fled the chamber and deflated with deep sighs of relief as soon as the study doors thudded closed behind them.

None of the four spoke as they returned to their rooms. The colleges were on the far side of the Guild above the riverbank. The apprentices cut through the gardens to reach them, crossing the small lake on one of the long bridges that arced over the mirrored surface. The sun had turned the western sky into a white haze above the Guild's rooftops, and the lake reflected the thick, wooly clouds that gathered like a herd of curious sheep every afternoon, their shining white tops leaping high above the somber coolness of their bases.

In the center of the lake rose the tall pillars of the Garden Palace, the wide amphitheater and its soaring, domed roof seated on top of a tinkling stream that cascaded down steps on every side, so that the Palace appeared to sit atop a bubbling fountain.

Beyond the garden the apprentices passed through a series of smaller courtyards and narrow passageways between buildings of every shape and size imaginable, tumbling over each other as if they had been cast onto the top of the hill from the hand of a giant who played at dice. These were the colleges, dozens of rambling houses and halls where the apprentices and masters lived and studied, each college fiercely proud of its heritage and customs.

Rikard navigated the maze with practiced ease and soon found the white walls and tall, thin towers of Killian College, named for the king who had endowed it eight hundred years ago.

The porter was gone from the gates and the quadrangle was empty, but that was not surprising given the hour. The apprentices hurried to the southeast corner, where they had been given a squat tower to live in.

A narrow staircase led to the first floor, where the tower's tiny study looked over the slate rooftop of the main hall of the college. Tall portraits of the college's illustrious past lined the stairs, white hair and master's robes framing stares of stern disapproval. The wooden stairs creaked at every step, a different well-known cry for each one, despite the worn runner which cascaded down them, its original color lost save at its un-trod edges.

Theirn pushed open the door to the study and gratefully sagged into one of the lumpy reading chairs next to the small fireplace. "Maker's breath, what the fuck was that?"

Rikard walked to the window and pushed out the iron-bound frame, latching the rod on its furthest notch. Fresh air slowly curled into the study, stirring the heavy dread that filled the room. Rikard took deep breaths, then frowned as anger began to push its way through relief.

"Apostate?" Theirn continued. "We didn't do anything."

"He just meant for us to be quiet," Clément said softly, "which is no different from anything else we are taught."

"It's different enough that the grandmaster told us personally," Theirn insisted.

"That just means it's important," Clément decided, "and it shouldn't matter, because we knew that already. He was just reminding us."

"It's different." Theirn shook his head. "It's different when the grandmaster tells you you're dead if you talk. You know it is."

"I know I have work to do," Clément replied, and he began arranging books and a collection of minute tools on the scarred surface of the table in front of him. "So do you."

Theirn snorted and shook his head in disgust, but abandoned the argument in favor of a ponderous tome. The study grew hushed, with only the dry rustle of Theirn's pages turning, and the soft taps of Clément's tools against the table's wooden top. Rikard knew he should be studying as well, as the day had mostly passed and Quentin was unlikely to forgive a lack of progress based only on a short time spent in the grandmaster's study, but Rikard had no patience for dry lessons on the melting points of various alloys. *Studying now would be a waste of time,* he reasoned with himself. He left the study and descended the creaking stairs, intending to go to the dining hall, but once he reached the quad he stopped, as uninterested in food as he was in study. His mind was restless, shying away from mundanity as it sought some resolution to the events of the day.

Rikard sat against one of the pillars in the colonnade, watched the shadows of the college's towers creep across the wide courtyard, and wrestled with discontentment.

Light footsteps approached and Dominique appeared beside him. She watched in silence for a moment, then sat as well, with her knees tucked under her chin and her arms wrapped around her shins, and rocked gently back and forth on her pointed toes.

"Are you all right?" she asked quietly.

"Me?" Rikard was surprised. "Yes, I'm fine. Just… well, disappointed I suppose."

"It doesn't feel right, does it? Forget and back to work."

"No," Rikard agreed. "Something special happened, right in front of us, and we'll never know what it was."

Dominique nodded. "I think he was frightened."

"Who was?"

"Grandmaster Dorian."

"Dorian was frightened? Of what?"

"Maybe he read something in that book on his desk. I'm not sure of what, but he was scared. I think that's why he called us in to threaten us himself."

"Wonderful. He's frightened, so we get threatened with apostate."

"Does it make you curious?"

Rikard glanced at Dominique. She was gazing at him out of the corner of her eye, waiting patiently, but he wasn't sure what to say.

"Curious? Of course I am, but I'm not curious enough to get branded an apostate. This isn't breaking curfew."

"No, I'm not curious enough, either," Dominique agreed quickly, and she dropped her gaze to her toes. "Maybe just enough to do a little research in the library. Nothing forbidden."

"I don't know, Dominique. Dorian didn't seem like he wanted us to know *anything* about the Gaze."

"He didn't say that. He said don't tell anyone."

Rikard frowned. "That sounds like playing with fire."

"No, it's learning about fire, so that we don't get burned. Don't you want to know what it is we are supposed to be cautious about?"

"It's too dangerous, Dominique." Rikard tried to catch her gaze, but she continued to watch her toes. "Promise me that you won't do anything."

Dominique laughed. "Promise you? Rikard, you don't even believe yourself."

"Yes, I do," Rikard said sternly.

"Maybe you do, right now, but you won't when you wake up tomorrow."

"Dominique, listen, Dorian didn't sound like he was kidding. I'm trying to be smart about this."

"I know you are, and it's sweet." Dominique hopped to her feet and brushed off her robes. "So I promise I won't do anything until tomorrow. Then we can do it together." She flashed a quick smile and strolled into their tower.

Rikard chuckled to himself and leaned back against his pillar again. *She said I was sweet.* His smile grew broader and he watched the sky slowly darken with a sense of complete contentment.

I, Aldric

The hushed shuffle of parchment and scratch of quills filled the main reading hall of the library as dozens of masters and apprentices engaged in the endless study required to devise, design, and craft Devices. Brilliant shafts of afternoon light speared into the hall through tall windows that dominated the far wall, so luminous that they appeared to be cast from polished gold. Only the dance of small motes of dust, each one glowing as if it were an ember from a fire, revealed their ethereal nature. Staircases spiraled up both walls of the room, their rails and steps wrought from iron shaped into elaborate flourishes and designs. The stairs led to long balconies along the walls, each one lined with tall shelves of books. Wheeled ladders needed to reach the highest shelves trundled busily along their ancient tracks, eternally patient as the researchers clambered up and down their worn steps.

Massive pillars marched down the center of the hall's wide floor, surrounded by heavy tables for the use of the library's occupants. Chandeliers on long chains hovered over the tables, and each one clutched a dozen small Diviners that emitted a soft, warm glow, although their light could hardly be noticed against the afternoon sun.

Rikard claimed an expanse of one of the massive tables by dropping his leather satchel on the polished mahogany surface, then climbed one of the soaring staircases to the third tier of shelves. The book he needed was a popular one, a treatise on metallurgy. The six copies made over the years were insufficient to serve the needs of the hordes of apprentices tasked with learning the basics of the craft that would occupy the remainder of their lives.

The newer copies were always gone, and today was no exception. But Rikard's favorite was there, a stained and faded volume whose scarred cover concealed the work of a scribe whose curiosity extended far beyond simple transcription. The writer had annotated the pages heavily with notes of his own, hints that reached beyond ores and heat and tempering, and explored the use of each metal in a Device. Only hints, and most of them indecipherable for an apprentice in his first year, but Rikard found them irresistible.

Rikard settled at the table and tried to concentrate on how the properties of base metals transformed as they were blended into an alloy, but his mind refused to focus. Instead, it returned over and again to the shining glory of Aldric's Gaze, and the beautiful image of it glimpsed on the grandmaster's desk.

I'd wager the Gaze has an interesting blend of ores, Rikard glared at the book, frustrated by yet another tantalizing comment from the scribe. Rikard tapped his quill on the sheet of blank parchment he had laid out for his notes, then rose from his chair and strode purposefully across the room before he could change his mind.

Rikard retrieved a massive tome from its table at the head of the room, a ponderous history of the Guild that he remembered contained a description of the construction of the Hall of Demonstration. He staggered to his table under the book's weight, eased its heavy cover open, and began to pour over the wide sheets of vellum, searching for any mention of Aldric's Gaze.

But as the brilliant shafts of sunlight burnished the foot of the eastern wall, Rikard dropped his quill on a parchment only half-filled with scribbled notes and sighed in frustration.

Useless. Hardly a mention of the Gaze. I need a better book. One like Dorian had on his desk.

Rikard hurried to the entrance hall and plunged into a small passage tucked beneath the sweeping marble stairs that flanked the imposing room. A dozen steps along the passage were the doors to the master's lodge, a suite of elegant rooms where the masters might read without the inconvenience of apprentices rustling around them. Rikard eased into the wood-paneled entrance to the lodge and gave the small bell resting on a pedestal within a tiny shake, sending a soft chime into the forbidden depths of the lodge.

A grumbling cough and shuffling footsteps announced the arrival of a grey-haired master with a long, drooping nose and boney fingers who glared disapprovingly at Rikard as he entered the room.

"Rikard, is it?" the master sniffed.

"Yes, Master Onfroi."

"And what can we do for you, Apprentice Rikard?"

"I need a finder, Master Onfroi, thank you."

"Do you, indeed."

"Yes, sir. I'm doing chromium, and I nced to find—"

"Yes, yes, very well. Wait here."

Rikard waited patiently as the master crept away. Another apprentice entered the lodge and Rikard exchanged a silent nod with him as they waited until Onfroi returned, bearing a small wooden box.

"Here we are," he announced. He opened the box and removed a small Device, a silver sphere no larger than a plum. Onfroi placed the Device in Rikard's palm, then took his time writing Rikard's name on the small piece of parchment tucked inside the box.

"Very well, Rikard," Onfroi dismissed him and turned to the other apprentice. "Emile, is it?"

"Yes, Master Onfroi. I need a finder, sir."

"Do you, indeed…"

Rikard quickly left the lodge and returned to his spot at the reading table. He placed the Device on his open palm, and took a steadying breath, trying to quell the excitement that trembled in his fingertips. The finder was a Diviner, created for bumbling apprentices who knew nothing about empowering a Device, but its elementary Word was the product of an elegant, intricate design. It was, to Rikard's mind, a *real* Device, and one that he could empower.

He took another deep breath, but it was no use. A smile crept uncontrollably across his lips as he prepared the Word. *This is what it's all about.* Rikard had dreamt about adepts and their Devices since he was too young to remember, had invented Devices of world-shattering power in his daydreams, and had imagined himself wielding the Weapons of legend more times than could be counted. His dreams had led him to the Guild, and his passion had not been dampened by the discovery that he struggled with even the simplest of Words.

I can do this one, he grinned to himself. He assembled it carefully in his thoughts, clean and precise as an arch, and whispered it to the finder. Rikard felt the Word flow through him into the Diviner, and the tiny sphere quivered on his palm. Its surface opened like the shell of a beetle, gracefully withdrawing to reveal its delicate interior. Intricate threads of gossamer metal stirred, twining about each other in a spinning dance. A thin band of gold that encircled the finder pulsed with soft light, then waited, expectantly, for Rikard's command.

"I'm looking for a book that explains all about Aldric's Gaze," he told the Device. "Like the one Grandmaster Dorian had on his desk."

The gold circle of the finder brightened, soft pulses of light flashing and dimming until the entire ring throbbed with the glow. *Too many,* Rikard realized. Several of the patches of light were more luminous than the others, however, so Rikard chased after them, following them around the finder's ring as he stalked the library's tall shelves, until one after another the books were tracked down and carried to the table. When the five brightest glows had been obtained, Rikard let the finder close and carefully tucked it into his bag for safekeeping.

Then he began reading, his quill once again poised over his parchment, ready to pounce on whatever hidden knowledge was about to be revealed.

His first sheet was covered in scrunched scribbles and set aside to dry, and a second already half-filled, when a shadow loomed across the page.

"We've been thinking," Theirn announced as he dropped onto the chair next to Rikard.

"Have you?" Rikard put down the quill and leaned into the rigid back of the chair, massaging his fingers.

Dominique slid into the chair on the other side of Rikard and nodded her head in agreement. "We have, and we decided that finding out a bit more about Aldric's Gaze wouldn't hurt anything."

"Just as an academic pursuit, you see," added Theirn.

"I did sort of spend the afternoon in, um, academic pursuits, already," Rikard admitted with a sheepish grin. He slid his parchments across the table and offered them to the other apprentices. "It was only Beauregard's Compendium and a few other books a finder pointed out, but they do mention the Gaze several times. Mostly useless, but the older chapters made a few references that I didn't understand."

"Fantastic!" Theirn beamed. Then he frowned and pointed to the second word on the parchment he had been offered. "What does that say? Is this even Venaissine?"

"It says 'idiot.' And this word says 'Theirn.' Look, you can see the little droopy 'T,' right here."

"Just tell us what you found, or else we'll be here past supper trying to decipher your scribbling."

"Not much, unfortunately. The Gaze was made by Grandmaster Aldric, not just named after him, and it was placed in the Hall of Demonstration on the first day the Hall was opened. Apparently, Aldric was already dead by then because one of these books mentioned there was a remembrance for him at the ceremony. So, somehow Aldric died between empowering the

Gaze and having it placed in the Hall. The rest of it is either more of the same, or it doesn't make sense."

"What doesn't make sense?" Dominique asked.

"For example, I found a reference in the minutes of the Assembly, several decades after the war. Grandmaster Évarice, whoever that is, became extremely angry and went on a tirade in front of the Assembly. Here, this is a quote… 'Why do we wait and watch the Gaze while Duibhir sits in the tower that we built for him? Demand that he reveals where he has hidden the Guardian, or suffer our displeasure.' Apparently, Évarice's opinion was popular because his motion was defeated by only one vote."

"The Gaze was watching for a Guardian? Who is Duibhir?"

"No idea." Rikard shrugged. "You can see why I said it's hard to understand."

"The history books aren't going to tell us what the Gaze actually does, are they? We need a book like the one Dorian had, one that actually describes how it works," Dominique said.

"Yes, I had the same thought, but the problem is that the Gaze has been around forever, and the finder is overwhelmed. It points in every direction. There must be hundreds of books to read through."

"A finder can locate any book in the library," Dominique laughed.

"Yes, I do know that," Rikard said testily.

"Maybe the book we want isn't in the library," Theirn said thoughtfully. "A book like that might be in the archives."

"It's possible, but what I meant was that if the finder isn't showing you the way to the proper book, it's because you're not using it correctly," Dominique laughed again.

"It glowed and everything," Rikard protested.

"Yes, but if it pointed out books that didn't have what you wanted in them, then you used it incorrectly."

"You can have a go if you want." Rikard dug through his bag and held the finder out to Dominique.

"You can do it," Dominique assured him. "Just think about what you really want to find."

Rikard hesitated for a moment, unwilling to risk failure in front of the other apprentices. Then he shrugged and took a deep breath. He spoke the Word, and the finder readied itself.

Now, what do I really want to find? Rikard knew the words he spoke to the finder did not matter. The Device listened to his intent through his Word. Whatever he said was merely a way to help him shape his thought. *What did I say last time? A book about the Gaze. Dominique is right… that's not what I want to know. I want to know how it works.*

"I'm looking for a book that explains what Aldric's Gaze does."

The finder thrummed as it began its search, but no golden glow appeared in its ring.

"Maybe Theirn is right—" Rikard began, but then the finder pulsed and a single bright light shone from it.

The finder led them down narrow stairs and into a low passageway lined with squat pillars that appeared to bulge under the weight of the edifice above. What little space was left between the pillars was packed with shelves filled with books and scrolls. The tomes spilled out onto the floor in wobbly stacks where the shelves were not ample enough, or sat in hopeful rows, as if awaiting some kindly hand to lift them en mass to a newly cleared home above.

Another passageway, equally overrun, meandered to Rikard's left, and doorways littered the walls of both passageways at unpredictable intervals. Light the color of dust poked into the passage on one side, but the dim shafts did little but thicken the shadows beyond them into utter darkness.

Tiny, brass lanterns hung on hooks at the bottom of the stairs, and the apprentices quickly lit three to carry with them. The finder's glow was steady and sure as they threaded their way down the passageway, cautious not to brush against the precarious stacks of books. The finder suddenly took them left, through a narrow gap between shelves that concealed a side passage, then left again, through a small chamber packed with barrels of scrolls, then right, down an even narrower passageway. Here, it sought out an alcove on the right, a cramped space with a low ceiling between two of the thick pillars, filled with crates of all sizes. A single shaft of grey light stabbed the floor through a recessed window no larger than a dinner plate, doing little more than revealing the clouds of dust that swirled into the air with every movement the apprentices made.

Rikard stepped into the alcove and slowly swung the finder in an arc as he watched the Device's steady glow. The golden light remained anchored on a small box resting on a ledge below the window. Rikard set his lantern down and cautiously picked the box up. A bright chime of metal striking stone cascaded down the wall to the floor, and Rikard stooped low and peered into the shadows until he found the telltale gleam of a small key that had certainly rested under the box until the apprentice had scraped it off its perch. Rikard set the box on top of one of the larger chests in the room, and fit the small key to the box's filigree-encrusted lock. The key turned easily and there was the click of metal releasing.

Rikard paused with his thumb on the latch.

"What's the wager? Aldric's head?"

"His prick?" Theirn laughed.

"Maker's breath," Dominique rolled her eyes to the ceiling in frustration. "Little boys."

Rikard grinned unapologetically and opened the box with a dramatic flourish. The three apprentices peered into its interior. A bundle of rich cloth lay carefully wrapped around a small object, nestled against the plushly padded lining of the box. Rikard unfolded the fabric, revealing a book with an elegant binding of engraved silver and gilded pages so smoothly cut that Rikard had to pass a finger over their edges to make sure they were parchment leaves.

Rikard removed the book from its home and placed it on the large chest the apprentices were using as a table. The book opened easily under the lightest of touches, and Rikard cautiously turned a few pages, so thin that he could see the shadow of his fingers through them. Each page was covered in dense writing and carefully rendered diagrams drawn in a meticulous, precise hand. The ink had faded to tawny beige in places, making it hard to read, but in others, it remained crisp and black.

Rikard returned to the first page and stared at the first two words written there, larger and bolder than the rest. 'I, Aldric…'

"Well, it's a book…" Theirn chuckled, and Rikard realized he had been holding his breath as he grinned in response.

"Looks like it's his private journal," Rikard guessed, turning the pages. "It isn't a transcription, look, you can see where he has gone back and made corrections and changed things."

"This should be in the archives," Dominique mused. "Not stuck down here."

"I would wager that there's a fancy copy written by a scribe in the archives, and they forgot about the original," Theirn replied.

"Whatever the reason, I'm glad," Rikard decided. "Let's get out of here before someone comes by."

They replaced the box on the window ledge, stashed the journal in Rikard's bag, and hurried to the main level.

"Do we read it here, or…?" Theirn asked, gazing around the crowded chamber.

"No. Back to college," Dominique said firmly. "I want to take my time with this, not be worried about being seen by a nosey master."

They strolled casually through the imposing library doors and across the grounds to Killian college, but Rikard's heart did not stop pounding until they had closed their tower door firmly behind them. They raced up the stairs to the study and quickly cleared a patch of table. Rikard reverently placed the journal on the scarred wood and the apprentices huddled over it.

"Find a picture of the Gaze," Theirn suggested.

Rikard nodded and began to turn the pages. Every one bore some diagram or design on it, from intricate renderings of branches and leaves, to detailed examinations of runes and bindings, to musings on the shapes of clouds and waves. But most common of all were the sketches of Devices, drawn in exquisite detail with few corrections. Many bore no explanation, but were simply islands immersed in the flow of words around them.

The first pages of the journal gave way to a section dedicated to architecture, and the apprentices saw designs for many of the Guild buildings grow and take shape on the pages before them. Then, finally, the shape they had been hunting for.

Aldric had consumed several pages with his sketches of the Gaze, but the images were unsupported by any explanation of what the apprentices were staring at. A few words or abbreviations marked the diagrams, but otherwise, the pictures stood alone on the page. Then, finally, on the page with the last picture of the Gaze, a few terse sentences written in a fierce scrawl.

Rikard read the words several times in growing confusion and met the puzzled gazes of Theirn and Dominique.

"Who is Lazarre?" Rikard asked.

"I don't know," Dominique admitted. She frowned at the open page. "I don't think Aldric liked him, whoever he was. Look… 'his idiotic betrayal'… 'great folly'… oh, and 'may he rot in the Grave.' Not exactly friendly."

"No," Theirn agreed. "The rest isn't helpful either. What is he talking about?"

" 'The Source is once again complete, but they have placed it within the Guardian and hidden it from us,' " Rikard read. "Cryptic, isn't it, except we have 'Guardian', again. Oh, and here he's upset that 'They have concealed the Blade as well.' Is this even talking about the Gaze at all?"

"I don't know." Dominique shook her head in frustration. "There's a lot of hidden things. Maybe the Gaze is searching for them?"

"Could be." Rikard ran his fingers through his hair, trying to push away his confusion. "And then there's this… 'the Vessel is gone. She is dead, and the fools worship her sacrifice. A new Vessel must be found if the Source is to be contained.' Martyr's tears, this is useless. Does he explain any of this?"

"Why would he?" Theirn asked. "He's writing for himself."

"We have to read the whole thing," Dominique decided. "From the beginning."

***

Their candles had melted to nubs by the time Rikard finally rose from the table and pressed his palms into his weary eyes. He twisted the ache in his shoulders away and dragged himself to the stove to make some tea.

Theirn lay curled into one of the reading chairs by the small fireplace, snoring contentedly, until the telltale whistle of the battered kettle summoned him awake.

Dominique accepted her tea gratefully and took it to the window. She gazed through the ancient panes at the night-black sky, gently blowing away the curls of steam from the surface of her cup.

Rikard stared at the journal, still open on the table, his stomach churning with excitement and dread. The silence in the room stretched heavily, with only the creak of the slowly cooling kettle to disturb it.

"We will need Clément," Theirn ventured, "for the door."

Dominique nodded. "Go and wake him up, then." She returned her attention to the window. "He is not going to like this."

Theirn departed and returned quickly with Clément in tow. The thin apprentice showed no signs of having been recently awakened and was dressed in an immaculate robe of embroidered cotton. Only his bare feet gave away his recent slumber.

Clément read silently, turning each page with a precise flip of his fingers. When it became obvious that Clément was not going ask any questions, Rikard claimed another of the reading chairs and gave in to eyelids heavy with exhaustion.

When at last Rikard was awakened by a kick to his leg, the room had turned grey with the light of dawn.

"He's done," Theirn told him, and Rikard struggled out of the chair and rubbed his face vigorously to banish the clinging blankets of warm slumber.

Dominique handed Rikard a cup of steaming tea, and they joined Clément at the table.

"What do you think?" Theirn asked without preamble.

"It is certainly interesting," Clément granted. "But I do not really see the urgency. Even if this is true, it happened one thousand years ago."

"*If* it's true?" Theirn's eyebrows shot upward, and he stared at Rikard and Dominique for support.

"Of course," Clément continued, unperturbed. "You have no idea of the provenance of this journal. Yes, it certainly reads as if the author were Grandmaster Aldric, but there is nothing to corroborate it. For the sake of discussion, however, I will grant you its origins. Then what?"

"Then… we've found out that the Guild created the Crunorix." Theirn spread his hands in bewilderment. "That's all. Did you read the same journal as the rest of us?"

"I did, and you are being dramatic," Clément frowned. He tapped the journal with a long, elegant finger as he made his points. "The journal claims that Aldric is not, in fact, the founder of the Guild and the creator of the Forge, but that it was this man, Lazarre, and Aldric was merely one of his disciples."

"And…" Theirn urged.

"And the rest is unclear."

"That's not fair, Clément," Dominique said quietly. "Some of what Aldric wrote is difficult to understand, and some of it is hard to hear, but what he is saying is not unclear."

"I think you are being generous."

"How so?" Theirn demanded. He opened the journal and flipped quickly through the pages until he found the one he wanted, then jabbed at the text with his finger. "What does that say?"

" 'Lazarre tells me that he has discerned a schism in the Source, that its singular divinity is, in fact, two, equally balanced, merged while they are contained within the Vessel. One he has named Creation. The other, he will not name. It is this one Lazarre insists speaks to the essence of life itself. He claims to be able to draw it forth, to use it to empower his new Device, but I sense only shadow and darkness in his words.' "

"And…" Theirn flipped toward the front of the journal with no regard for the delicate pages. He stabbed his finger onto another passage. "Here."

" 'Lazarre has disregarded our warning, he is deaf to our pleas.' " Clément read easily, his voice elegant, and Rikard could practically hear the tones of the ancient Grandmaster if he closed his eyes. " 'Lazarre has torn the Source from the Vessel, and the Forge is to be cast aside. Already it stands cold and dark. All sacrificed for one Device. Lazarre claims it will lead us to true power, but all I see is our ruin.' "

"What about… here."

" 'They are all gone, all twelve of them. Only I remain to face the High King. They call themselves the Crunorix, now, while I am Grandmaster of a corpse. There is, perhaps, one slim chance. Lazarre did not take the Source from the Vessel, he tore it in half. The Forge cannot use it, but perhaps there is a way. It is something to offer the High King. I hope it is enough.' "

"Do I need to keep on?" Theirn challenged Clément. "How can you say this isn't clear?"

"Because it isn't," Clément insisted. "It is just hearsay and vague assertions."

"Ohhh, Clément," Dominique groaned. "Honestly, just because there aren't any corroborating sources doesn't mean it's unclear. There won't be, not for this sort of thing."

"Regardless," Clément continued hurriedly, and Rikard saw a tinge of red appear over Clément's cheekbones at Dominique's rebuke. "I have already said I will grant you the content, which brings us to the urgency. If this is all true, it happened a millennium ago, and Aldric did a good job of getting rid of a cancer within the Guild and preserving the Guild for us today. Why are we up in the middle of the night for that?"

"Because of Aldric's Gaze," Rikard told Clément.

"I guessed it would come around to the Gaze," Clément frowned at his companions. "You all swore you would not pursue the Gaze."

"There was no chance of that," snorted Theirn, "and it's a good thing we did."

"Why?"

"Think about this," Rikard urged Clément. "Ruric's war was barely over, a war that Aldric knows was started by Lazarre and the other Guild Grandmasters. However he did it, Aldric fixes the Forge and gets High King Ruric to trust the Guild, and the war is won. Now, what is the first thing Aldric does? He builds the Gaze. He's just helped defeat the Crunorix, he's just saved the Guild, and he wants to find…"

"There are the things he listed on the page with the Gaze's design. The hidden Guardian, the concealed Blade. A new Vessel."

"Yes, perhaps. I think he would want to know if his enemy is still out there."

"The Crunorix."

"Yes, absolutely," Rikard stated.

"You think the Gaze is telling us that the Crunorix have returned."

"Worse than that." Rikard glanced at Theirn and Dominique, and they nodded their approval to continue. "I think they've never left. I think they're here."

"What?" Clément shook his head, baffled. "Perhaps I did indeed read a different book than you."

"Well, just listen a bit," Rikard continued in a rush, hoping he sounded reasoned and calm, instead of frantic, as he feared. "The Crunorix *were* the Guild. Yes, eleven of the grandmasters left with Lazarre, but who knows how many more there were. Aldric would want to conceal that, and he would want to get rid of the rest as quickly as he can, so he builds the Gaze. But he dies suddenly, within days of completing the Gaze."

"You are saying he was murdered."

"That's right."

"And the Gaze is sounding the alert now because…"

"Because the Crunorix are not hiding anymore. Whatever they've been doing all this time, they're coming out of hiding."

"Here, in the Guild?"

"Yes, here. They never left. That's why Dorian was so furious that we'd seen the Gaze."

"Now you are saying that Grandmaster Dorian is a secret Crunorix."

"It makes sense. Why else would he threaten us with apostate just for seeing the Gaze go off?"

"Well, if you are right about the Gaze's function, it seems more likely that Dorian would want to keep the truth of the Crunorix's origins hidden, or perhaps simply make sure the Crunorix are not alerted to the fact that they have been discovered. Really, it's extremely far-fetched, all of it. You are creating a grand conspiracy out of a long-ago death we know nothing about and the fact that Dorian was tetchy the other day. He's always tetchy."

"Threatening us with apostate is more than tetchy," Theirn pointed out.

"He was just making a point." Clément shook his head. "Look, it is all fascinating, but there is no way to know."

"Yes, there is," Rikard said. "If we can find out for certain what the Gaze is doing, we will know."

"How will we do that?" Clément laughed. "I examined those diagrams in the journal. There is no chance we will be able to decipher the Gaze from those. It is far beyond anything I have seen, or can understand, I know that."

"We need more," Rikard agreed. "We need books like the one on Grandmaster Dorian's desk."

"And how exactly… you want to sneak into Dorian's study. And do what? Read a few pages by candlelight and somehow learn all about using one of the most intricate Devices ever crafted? Or was your plan to copy the entire book in a single night?"

"We just have to find out what it does," Rikard said reasonably. "If it's what we think, then we go on to the next step."

"Which is what?"

"Well…" Rikard turned the pages of the journal until he found the image he was searching for. "We open this."

Clément shook his head. "You *are* insane. Even if that is the same as the one in Dorian's study, opening it will definitely get you thrown out, perhaps even branded apostate. In any case, how will you open it? Have you suddenly turned adept when I was not watching?"

"No." Rikard grinned. "You could do it."

Clément sat back, speechless, as he stared at first one and then the other of his fellow apprentices.

"The Word isn't that bad," Rikard continued reasonably. "Even I can make out parts of it."

"Martyr's tears, you are serious."

"Clément, look, you're right, a short glimpse at a book won't do us much good. We must find more, and there's really only one place where those secrets are kept. That's where we need to go, and we need your help to get there. You're the only one of us who has a chance with that Word."

"The only one of *us*? I do not even believe you. Go and find someone who does and ask them."

"You know we can't do that," Dominique said gently. "If we are right, we can't trust anyone. If we are wrong, we will find out and there's no harm. Clément, I know you may not agree with us, but if we're right…"

Clément shook his head, his mouth a thin line as he glared at the table in front of him. Long moments passed, and then he held out his hand to Rikard. "Let me see that Word."

Rikard grinned and gladly handed Clément the journal.

Pain and Death

The Hall of Demonstration slowly filled with the dignified ranks of the Guild masters. Long robes covered in rich embroidery and precious metal swished softly on the polished wood floor, and the ancient benches creaked under the weight of so many dignified posteriors.

Apprentices packed into the small gallery above the doors to the Hall, fidgeting under the weight of their formal robes as they waited for the long procession below to end.

At the head of the Hall, the tall alcove that had housed Aldric's Gaze stood empty, although someone had hung a rich tapestry on its back wall, apparently dissatisfied by the blank stone left by the absence of the Gaze.

At last, the masters were settled on their red cushions and the muffled rustling stilled. The doors to the Hall swung open, and three initiates entered, dressed in black robes with gold embroidery and voluminous hoods that concealed their faces in shadow. The initiates solemnly walked the length of the Hall under the gaze of the masters and, with heads bowed, took their places on the dais that stood in the center. A master closed the small gate that led to the dais with a sharp click that sounded clearly across the hushed Hall.

Grandmaster Dorian rose from his place on the lowest row of benches and walked majestically to the end of the Hall, followed by the most senior of the masters.

While the eyes of the Guild were on the stately procession of its leaders, the small door at the back of the gallery opened slightly and four apprentices slipped out.

They hurried through the deserted hallways that skirted the balcony and down the stairs to the empty atrium.

The resonate chorus of the Guild masters acknowledging the initiates echoed into the atrium as a muffled murmur, just loud enough to hide the quick scuffle of the apprentices' sandals and the swish of their formal robes as they scurried across the atrium and plunged down a long hallway.

At the far end, a short stair gave access to the lowest floor of the Hall of Demonstration, and the apprentices slowed to a rather more dignified walk, as a precaution against the unexpected appearance of a master.

But the hallway remained deserted, and the apprentices soon found the passage they sought. A short hall, barely longer than it was wide, featureless save for a line of narrow windows high on one wall.

Rikard ran his hand over the smooth, white plaster that formed the flat end of the hallway. It was cool to the touch, and as smooth as glass.

"Once you know it's there, it's obvious, isn't it?" Theirn said thoughtfully.

"Is it." Rikard frowned at Theirn skeptically. "It's plastered over completely. There's not even the tiniest hint."

"Well, no," Theirn admitted, "but you can tell from the shape of the wall. It's obvious."

"For a thousand years, no one has noticed, but to him it's obvious," Rikard appealed to the others for support against Theirn's claim.

"If Aldric had not sketched the door in his journal, you would have never guessed," Clément sniffed. "Never."

"Can we hurry?" Dominique said impatiently. "We don't have all night. Dorian will be busy for a while, but he won't chant forever."

Clément concentrated briefly, and Rikard felt the faintest whisper of a Word brush against his mind. The plaster in the center of the wall suddenly cracked, and a small shower of dust crumbled free from the smooth surface.

"There is the latch," Clément said with a satisfied smile. He probed the small hole in the plaster with one long finger, then pressed firmly. There was a metallic click and then the quiet rumble of gears within the wall. For a moment, Rikard wondered if the door would open or if a combination of centuries of disuse and a liberal application of plaster had disabled it. Then the wall shattered. The plaster cracked and fell free in wide chunks that exploded into dust on the floor, revealing the carved stone surface of the hidden door swinging into a narrow passage beyond.

"Martyr's tears," Theirn laughed as the door slowly came to a rest against the passage wall. "I think there's a chance they might notice this."

"Then let's hurry," Rikard said. "We won't get another chance at this, that's for certain."

The apprentices swept as much of the rubble into the passage as they could. With the door closed behind them and the debris concealed, there was hope that an uninterested glance into the disused hall would not notice the appearance of a small door where there had not been one for centuries, nor the ragged plaster hole in which it was framed.

They pulled tiny lanterns from their robes and Rikard led the way into the passage. The light revealed unadorned stone bricks and a low, arched ceiling that forced Rikard to walk hunched over. They paused only long enough for Clément to seal the door behind them, then they scurried into the darkened tunnel.

The door was soon swallowed by the darkness behind them. The glow of the small lanterns illuminated only a few steps ahead and the tunnel appeared blocked by a black mist that retreated only as fast as Rikard could stride toward it.

But before Rikard could fill the darkness ahead with the demons of childhood stories there was a small gleam of light in the distance, and then another, and soon the lanterns revealed the steel bars that secured the door at the far end of the passage.

Rikard unlatched the door and carefully stepped on the release plate, and the door swung easily inward with a soft grumble.

"Oh," Rikard said, puzzled. The opening of the tunnel was covered in planks of dark wood, completely blocking it. He ran the lantern around the doorway, searching for a knob. Rikard tried a gentle shove and was rewarded by a chorus of chimes and the clink of glass as the wooden wall shifted.

"What is going on?" Theirn asked.

"I think they put a shelf in front of the door," Rikard decided. He pushed again, lower, and the wooden wall shifted across the floor with a long scrape. The clash of glass and metal was much louder this time, and Rikard held his breath, wondering if there was anyone to hear on the other side of the door.

There was no shout of alarm, however, and Rikard slid the shelf aside with a series of careful shoves until there was room to squeeze through the gap.

He found himself at the end of a long room lined with alcoves, filled with the whir and ting of a thousand tiny gears. Tall shelves stood in each alcove, bearing dozens of small, intricate Devices made of glass, crystal, and precious metal. Rikard brought the lantern close to the Devices that he had nearly tipped onto the floor, and gave a low whistle of astonishment.

"Timepieces," he murmured to Clément as the tall apprentice joined him. The intricate structures were far more than the wonders of weights, springs, and gears that made up a mundane timepiece, as marvelous as those instruments were. These timepieces were Devices, Diviners that were crafted to discern much more than simply the time of day, and would do that task with a preternatural precision. "Look at them all."

"Astonishing," Clément agreed.

"Are any of them the Gaze?" Theirn asked.

"No," Rikard decided.

"Then stop playing with them," Dominique whispered. "We do not have much time."

"Let's see, I can tell you exactly..." Rikard peered at the nearest timepiece. It was crafted in the shape of a fierce dragon made of silver with diamond eyes, curled around a dark gem that had a red tinge in the lantern's light. The dragon was intent on eating its own tail, and most of its sinuous body had already disappeared down its gullet. As Rikard watched, the dragon swallowed another mouthful of silver scales and clamped its teeth a finger's-width further along its body. "The dragon says we are half-way between sunset and midnight. Oh! That's what he's holding in his claws. It's the moon. Waxing gibbous tonight. Apparently."

"Does it have a marking for when Grandmaster Dorian returns to his quarters?" Dominique asked sweetly.

"Ummm, no," Rikard reported.

"Then leave it!" she hissed emphatically, and stalked from the room.

Rikard and Clément followed, chastened. "Where do you suppose its tail goes?" Rikard asked quietly, but Clément only shook his head in bafflement.

The room filled with timepieces led to a wide hallway decorated with stiff chairs and grand paintings. At the end of the hall, sweeping windows overlooked the gardens and allowed silver shafts of moonlight into the hall. Rikard recognized a pair of polished doors along the side of the hall, and he felt a thrill of excitement.

"Those are the doors to Dorian's study."

"I can't believe it worked," Clément said in disbelief.

"Come on," Theirn laughed softly. "Let's go and find those books."

Theirn pushed the doors open and the apprentices crept into the shadowy room beyond. Moonlight blazed on the wide, polished desk, and the pillars threw black pools of darkness in long lines across the room.

Rikard carefully crossed the room to the desk, but stopped as his gaze caught a shape against the wall.

"You see," Rikard whispered. He pulled Aldric's journal from his satchel and held it open triumphantly. On the open page was a diagram of a door, flanked by two ravens perched in alcoves, holding Diviners in their outstretched talons. "It *is* the same."

"Yes, you're very smart," Theirn assured him.

"Oh, no…" Dominique groaned in frustration. She glared at the pristine surface of the massive, black desk, with her fists clenched on her hips. "The books are gone."

"Does that mean we can leave?" Clément asked.

"No," all three of the other apprentices hissed in unison.

"Never mind about the books," Rikard insisted. "Yes, it would have been nice to finally find out how the Gaze works, but that's not why we are here. Not really."

"I do understand," Clément said coolly.

"If you understand, then why are you still arguing about it?" Theirn demanded.

"Because, as I have said, even if the journal is correct, I am not sure why that means we should be trying to break into the archives."

"Here, do you need to study the Word again?" Rikard offered Clément the journal.

"I remember it," the tall apprentice responded. "Are you absolutely sure this is a good idea?"

"No," Rikard admitted, "but we will never be able to get into the archives through the main doors. I'm just glad Aldric decided the grandmaster needed a private entrance in his study."

"Very well." Clément faced the raven-flanked door and closed his eyes, his brows clenched in concentration. The room grew heavy in its silence, even the night song of the frogs in the garden below fading into anticipation. Rikard held his breath until he could hold it no longer, then did it again, and still Clément did not move, and the door did not open.

Rikard approached Dominique and they shared concerned glances. "It's not working," Rikard whispered to her.

"Give him a bit longer," Dominique decided.

"How much longer? We don't have forever."

"I know." Dominique glanced at the entrance to the study and clenched her arms tightly across her chest. "Just a bit."

Rikard nodded. He did not want to give up, but more than that he did not want to get caught. *If this doesn't work, we will find another way.*

Theirn snorted in annoyance and began to pace between the desk and the archway to the balcony, and the scuff, scuff, shuffle of his footsteps scraped across Rikard's strained nerves.

"A bit longer," Dominique whispered.

"Martyr's tears," Rikard groaned under his breath.

Clément whispered to the door, and Rikard felt the gentle twist of the Word thrum in his chest. The door slid soundlessly into the wall. Cool air sighed against the fabric of their robes, and Rikard suppressed a shiver as a chill ran across his skin.

"Well done," Rikard congratulated Clément, and the tall apprentice nodded his head wearily, a small smile lifting the corner of his lips.

"It's so dark," Dominique whispered, and Rikard nodded his agreement. The room beyond the door was utterly lightless, as if they had opened a portal to a chamber beneath the roots of an ancient mountain, pushed so far from the surface that it had never seen any color save for black. The seamless stone floor was illuminated for a few steps by the light from their lanterns, but then it too disappeared into shadow, far sooner than Rikard thought natural.

Rikard and Dominique quickly stripped off their formal robes, revealing the much less constricting apprentice robes they wore underneath.

"Don't lose these," Rikard instructed Theirn. "We'll need those to blend in when we go back.

"I remember," Theirn frowned as he took the folded pile from Rikard and Dominique.

"All right," Rikard muttered, and he held his lantern above his head. Their shadows shifted across the visible floor, but the darkness did not retreat.

Rikard glanced at Dominique, and she returned his gaze with wide eyes. But her lips were set in a resolute line, and she nodded her head in quick readiness.

"All right," Rikard repeated, and he took a steadying breath. "Don't let that door close."

"We won't," Clément assured him.

Rikard took a tentative step across the threshold. The light from his lantern crept across the floor, pushing slightly into the shadows, but it revealed nothing to either side. Dominique joined him, and together they took another step, and a third, until they were completely cocooned by shadows that gathered far closer to them than felt possible. Rikard swung his lantern from one side to the other as they walked, but only the small patch of stone at their feet was illuminated, less than a few strides would take to cover.

"Look," Dominique whispered. Rikard turned to follow her gaze and saw that the entrance had disappeared. Endless dark loomed where he had expected to see the bright outline of the doorway, although they had taken less than a dozen steps.

"This isn't right," Rikard muttered. He held his lantern high and slowly turned in a full circle, but could find no shape or landmark of any kind in any direction. "Where is everything?"

"I'm not sure, but if you keep on spinning around like that we won't know which way we came from," Dominique pointed out.

Rikard realized she was right. Even the stone floor was featureless, showing no indication of which direction the door lay. "Do you know?"

"Yes, I'm still pointing the way we came."

"You're sure?"

"No."

"Theirn?" Rikard called softly. The two apprentices listened intently, but Rikard heard nothing but the thud of his heartbeat in his ears. Sweat began to prickle his skin despite the cool, dry air, and he gulped down an urge to yell.

"Shit," Rikard whispered. "Do we go back? Or forward?"

"I don't think it matters. Forward."

They continued walking across the endless stone floor, forever pushing into the thick, dark shadows. Rikard experimented with leaving a quill on the floor. It vanished after only a few steps, but they could not find it when they retraced their path. Their pace increased after that, hurrying across the featureless stone until their breath came in ragged gasps.

"Ohhh, this is useless," Dominique declared, her voice rising in frustration. "We've walked half-way to Criénne. And now my lantern is practically out of oil."

"Mine, too." Rikard jostled the lantern and listened to the forlorn echo of the oil inside the brass reservoir. "We should have turned one off. How long have we been in here?"

"Too long. They must have finished the initiation by now." Dominique doused her lantern. "Check the journal again."

"It doesn't say anything about—"

"Just check it," Dominique insisted. "What other chance do we have? Keep walking until the lanterns are done and we sit here in the dark waiting for someone to find us? Or worse?"

"No," Rikard replied, and he dug into his bag and retrieved the small journal one more time. He did not think it likely that they would be left to starve to death. *Someone will notice two idiots trapped in the archives as soon as it's morning.* He was not sure that was any better. *It will be the Citadelle for us.*

Rikard glared balefully at the small journal in his hand. The faded ink swam in the dim light of his lantern as he slowly turned the thin pages, re-reading every convoluted phrase with fresh hatred. His lantern suddenly dimmed and flickered, and he gave it a fresh shake. This time there was no slap of oil against metal.

The scrape of Dominique's lighter was swallowed by the shadows as she re-lit her lantern. Rikard sighed and shook his head.

"There's nothing," he said hopelessly. "Or if there is, I can't find it."

Dominique pursed her lips angrily and began to pace, staring into the black shadows as if she were an animal in a cage, glaring at her captors.

"Theirn!" she shouted, "Clément!"

Rikard returned the journal to his bag, then closed his useless lantern and thrust it into the bag as well, where it clunked hollowly against something. Rikard frowned and dug angrily in the bag, ready to hurl whatever infuriating object he found into the shadows.

Then he laughed.

"What?" Dominique snapped.

"Nothing." Rikard laughed again. "I mean, it can't work, right? But look."

He held out the object that had banged against his lantern, a tiny ball of engraved silver.

"A finder," Dominique breathed softly. "No, it can't possibly…"

Rikard took a resolute breath and spoke the simple Word. The Device unfolded gracefully, revealing its heart of spinning rings. "Here," Rikard told it, and he aligned the Word with the small journal in his hand. "Where does this belong?"

The Device whirred softly as its rings accelerated, and a warm, golden light filled the engravings along one edge.

"I don't believe it," Rikard laughed.

"Come on, before it realizes what it's doing."

The apprentices hurried in the direction of the Diviner's glow. Ten steps brought them to a door set in a stone wall, looming so suddenly from the darkness that both Rikard and Dominique gasped and shied away from the dark shape. Rikard grinned sheepishly and was rewarded with a happy smile in return, and they approached the door.

The stone slab bore no handle or lock and was set almost seamlessly into the wall.

"Do you think it's the door back to Dorian's study?" Rikard asked, running his hand across the door's cold surface.

"It looks the same," Dominique murmured. "But why would Clément have closed it?"

"Maybe he had to? Maybe someone came to the study? Who knows, just see if you can open it."

Dominique nodded and ran her hand over the door's surface. Her fingertips brushed against the stone, and the door stirred, then slid into the wall with only the faintest of trembles felt through the floor. The chamber beyond was dark, but it was the darkness of space and cool quiet, so different from the oppressive weight of the thick shadows that Rikard nearly leapt through the doorway.

Small echoes of his footsteps drifted into immense space. Dominique's lantern revealed only that they stood on a small balcony with an ornate railing. A break in the railing gave access to a narrow bridge that arced into the chamber, but the dim light did not reach far enough to reveal the bridge's destination.

Faint streaks of shimmering light drifted through the darkness below the balcony, and at first, Rikard thought that he saw the reflection of the lantern from some polished metal, or perhaps a floating mist. But he quickly realized that the light extended far from the lantern's reach, and shifted with a gentle motion that had nothing to do with the lantern.

"Turn off the lantern," Rikard whispered. "Just for a moment."

Dominique did so without question, and they waited next to each other as the chamber slowly appeared around them.

A small bridge extended from their feet to the center of the room, wide enough for them to walk side-by-side. On either side of the bridge lay a wide pit, deep enough that Rikard guessed he would not be able to see out of it if he stood on its floor. Faint silver light washed across the bottom of the pit, glimmers that faded away virtually as soon as they appeared, but they provided enough illumination for Rikard to see that there was a thin layer of liquid at the bottom of the pit, likely no deeper than the length of a finger, and that the silver light danced on the surface of the liquid.

The apprentices walked slowly across the bridge toward the center of the chamber. Gossamer ripples of reflected light climbed the walls of the chamber, a stone's-throw away on either side, until they disappeared into obscurity in the shadows above.

In the center of the chamber, a massive tower rose from a circular platform. The tower was crafted out of a metal so black that Rikard could not make out its true shape in the shadows, but he could tell that its convoluted mass grew ever thicker as it ascended, with strange protrusions and hulking lumps looming in the darkness above their heads. At its base, the tower was no wider than Rikard's hand, and the apprentices approached it warily.

The surface of the platform sloped toward an angular dome that hulked in the center, directly beneath the tip of the tower. Only a hand's-breadth of empty air separated the two. The platform's stone was engraved with threads of polished metal, patterns far more intricate than any structure Rikard had ever seen in any Device.

"I think we are inside the Forge," Rikard whispered.

Dominique nodded silently, her eyes wide as she stared at the dome at the center of the platform.

"What do you see?" Rikard asked her.

"It has a lid. I think it opens."

She's right. The top of the dome was formed by a thick slab of stone, held precisely in place by a series of locks.

"Come on," Rikard muttered. He approached the dome, stepping cautiously along a thin strip of stone left free from the delicate circuits of the Device. The dome was larger than Rikard had thought at a distance, reaching his chest in height and much longer than his arms could stretch. Dominique bent close to one of the locks to examine it, then reached tentative fingers to touch it.

"What are you doing?" Rikard whispered.

"They twist to open," Dominique replied.

"Don't," Rikard urged. "Martyr's tears, Dominique, if they find out—"

"What? Rikard, we are inside the Forge. Not even the masters are allowed in here. If they catch us in the archives, it's the Citadelle for a few years, if we're lucky, forever if we're not. Caught in the Forge? That's us gone, vanished, disappeared. Do you understand? Do you think it will matter whether or not we open this thing?"

"No, but why—"

"Because, when they come to kill me, I don't want my last thought to be, 'I wonder what was inside that thing?' Rikard, it is not going to make a difference to them, and I do not want to die for seeing the *outside* of a box."

"Fair enough, but I don't want to die at all," Rikard hissed. "We should be finding a way out of here, not messing around."

"It will only take a moment," Dominique insisted. She twisted the lock under her fingers, and the circle of metal turned smoothly. "Especially if you help."

"Shit," Rikard muttered to himself. Then he hurried to release the locks on the other side of the lid, each one twisting open with a cold click.

With the locks released, the lid of the dome slid easily to the side, scraping gently against the stone base as it turned on hidden hinges buried beneath it. The inside was too dark to see, untouched by the soft light of the reflected water. Dominique lit her lantern with a snap, and its glow pulsed as she adjusted the flow.

The dome's interior was hollow, a nest of thin metal threads twisting around each other like the pale roots of a tree, each one covered in intricate markings. They surrounded an empty shape, the outline of a body, clearly delineated amongst the coiled roots. Long, segmented needles of metal clustered around the hollow like curled fingers, their tips gleaming in the lantern's light, poised next to where the body's head, arms, abdomen, and thighs would have lain. The bottom of the hollow was lined with rigid barbs, and in the center was a series of sunbursts of polished metal, their long rays interconnected, positioned from the crown of the head to the groin.

"Martyr's tears," Dominique whispered. "It looks like…"

It looks like pain and death. Rikard wanted to step away from the gaping hollow, to close the lid and lock it securely away again.

"Can you tell what it does?" Dominique asked.

"No," Rikard shook his head. "Not much, in any case. I've never seen anything like this before, and what we can see must just be a small part. It's clearly connected to the tower in some way, and it must go into the stone underneath us as well."

They examined the Forge together, long moments passing in silence as their eyes recorded details that their minds could not decipher, seeking any familiar clue in the patterns and finding none.

"I can't help but see a sarcophagus, now," Dominique said. She clutched her shoulders tightly and shivered. "I think we should go."

"All right," Rikard agreed, although his eyes lingered on the woven pattern of the metal roots within the hollow as he turned away. The lid closed as easily as it had opened, and it took only a moment to fasten the series of locks, but Rikard felt the passing of every heartbeat as if the next would never arrive.

With the sarcophagus closed they turned their backs on the central platform and hurriedly explored the narrow bridges that extended into the dark chamber at regular intervals around the center. Dominique doused her lantern again and they found their way by the ghostly light of the liquid in the pit, discovering that it revealed far more of the chamber, once their eyes had adjusted, than the tiny glow of the lantern.

Many of the bridges ended in small platforms against the wall, with doors identical to the one that they had entered through. But the doors would not open to their touch, and they were forced to retreat to the center of the chamber each time. Even the door they had come through was now closed, and as equally unresponsive, though they shoved and kicked it in frustration.

Finally, one bridge led to a much more massive platform in front of an imposing pair of doors that towered over the two apprentices. Embedded in the doors' stone were threads of metal that gleamed in the silver waves of light washing over them, forming patterns of intricate beauty. Rikard ran his fingers along the veins and realized that, for all his studies of the past year, he could only recognize how far he was from understanding what a Device could be.

The huge doors were as immovable as the small ones, and Rikard thumped them with his fist in frustration, producing no more than a soft slap of sound.

"Now what?"

"I don't know." Dominique frowned. "Perhaps there is a way up the tower?"

"We can look," Rikard said dubiously.

A thick, metallic tone sounded through the chamber, and the apprentices whirled to face the double doors. Sparks the color of lightning streaked across the doors' surface, intricate gears began to spin, and a faraway rumble sent trembles through the apprentices' sandals.

Rikard glanced desperately around the chamber, seeking any concealment. "Under the walkway," he gasped, and Dominique nodded quickly. They dropped into the pit, their sandals splashing in the scintillating water, and scurried under the span of the walkway as the doors split apart.

Rikard crouched against the stone pillar that supported the walkway, his head grazing the underside of the bridge. The ripples from their plunge still wavered on the surface of the liquid, but the rumble of the doors quickly overwhelmed the ripples with a dancing vibration that sent glimmers of light cascading in all directions. Dominique pressed against him as they huddled as close to the center of the bridge as possible, straining to hear over the thunder of the doors.

The doors came to a halt with a gentle thud, and the Forge gradually stilled as the echoes died away. Rikard held his breath. There was a sound lurking in the echoes. A high-pitched hum and a low roar of air being continuously drawn in. Then metal rustled against metal and heavy footsteps thudded into the walkway above Rikard's head, slow and purposeful. The sharp tang of hot metal washed over Rikard as the footsteps passed toward the center of the Forge.

Dominique's fingers tightened around Rikard's arm as she craned her head outward, and Rikard frantically signaled her to stop.

The footsteps paused at the end of the walkway, and again Rikard held his breath as he listened to the low roar that never ceased for any hint that the apprentices were about to be discovered. The pause stretched agonizingly until Rikard was forced to draw in a long, silent breath. Finally, the footsteps resumed, and passed over their heads once again, moving purposefully toward the door, and Rikard's shoulders sagged with relief.

"The door is open," Dominique breathed in his ear.

Rikard pushed his hair back from his forehead and nodded, although he wanted nothing more than to stay safely concealed until the doors were sealed again. *No, she's right. We need to get out of here, and we will never make it out the way we came.*

Rikard cautiously leaned around the edge of the walkway, ready to duck back in an instant if needed. He could not see the source of the heavy footsteps, but Rikard was happy to err on the side of caution. He edged around the pillar and crept along beneath the walkway, careful to ease into the liquid that lapped over his toes on every step. Dominique followed on his heels, the light touch of her fingers on his back the only sign that she was there.

They reached the end of the walkway, but there they would be forced to leave the concealment of the pool and clamber onto the platform if they wished to proceed. Rikard paused for a moment with his back to the wall, listening to the footsteps continue without pause until he judged that they had passed far enough away that they must be through the doorway. Then he turned and slowly raised to his full height and peered over the lip of the pool.

The doorway gaped open invitingly, the warm light from the antechamber on the far side bathing the platform in front of Rikard. The platform was empty, but Rikard hesitated, his eyes riveted on the figure silhouetted against the antechamber light. The light gleamed along the figure's edges, shining from layers of intricately overlapping metal. The figure was a head taller than Rikard, at least, and powerfully built, with wide shoulders and chest, and thick arms and strong legs. It held a tall lance in its left hand, the long shaft of the weapon flaring into a curved shield around the haft, but Rikard could discern little else in the shadows cast by the glaring lights behind the figure.

For a moment, Rikard was paralyzed, fearing that he had been seen. The figure was no more than a dozen steps in front of him, and there was no concealment along the edge of the platform. But the figure made no sign that it was aware of Rikard's presence, and Rikard suddenly realized that it was facing away.

Before the apprentice could breathe a sigh of relief, bright flames the color of lightning flared suddenly in the shadows across the figure's back, flickering against gleaming steel. The figure began to turn, and Rikard ducked below the platform's edge.

The sound of two heavy footfalls carried clearly to Rikard, then a pause as quiet as a deep well, and then the rising thunder of the doors gliding together. Rikard strained to hear any sound above the grumble of metal and stone. He was not sure how long it would take the doors to close, but the light from the antechamber was dimming with dismaying speed.

"We have to go," whispered Dominique.

"He's still there," Rikard hissed back.

"We'll have to run past him, then." Dominique's lips set in a firm line. "We can't just stay in here."

"There's no chance," Rikard insisted.

"Run fast, then. I'm not staying here, and I'm not going back into that room of shadows. I'm not."

Rikard slowly nodded his head. He could still feel the piercing terror of that cold, desperate place. *Anything is better than going back there.*

"Then I will go first. Wait for him to chase me, then you go."

"No. Help me up, then follow as fast as you can."

He cupped his hands for her foot and crouched. "Don't wait for me."

"If he chases me, you let him. Just get out, yourself."

"All right," Rikard lied. "Ready?"

Dominique nodded, placed one sandaled foot lightly into his hands, and balanced herself against him. Their faces were only a hand's-breadth apart, and Rikard saw that her pupils were wide and dark, and her fingers trembled on his shoulders. "Ready," she whispered.

Rikard braced to heave her upward, but hesitated. *I can't do this… I can't throw her up there by herself. She won't have a chance. This is insane.*

"Rikard… now," Dominique hissed, but Rikard knew he was not going to throw her to the wolves.

Before he could do more than open his mouth to reply, Rikard heard the sound that he had given up hope for, the deliberate tread of heavy steel on stone. For an instant, he felt sure that the footsteps were coming toward the edge of the platform, but after only a moment it was clear that the figure was moving steadily away from the doorway. The light from the antechamber was nearly gone, and Rikard knew they had only the briefest of time left before they were trapped.

He straightened and heaved against Dominique's slender weight, and she leapt gracefully out of his hands and landed on the platform. Rikard jumped after her and scrambled over the edge, his wet sandals slipping on the stone as Dominique pulled on his arms.

The doors were grumbling inexorably across the final arm's-length of open doorway.

"Come on!" Dominique urged as she began to run. Rikard launched himself after her and they sped across the platform.

They had time for the briefest of pauses in the rapidly diminishing doorway to peer into the antechamber. Rikard caught a glimpse of the armored figure marching away to their right, the blue flames licking across its back a beacon to Rikard's gaze, so the apprentices turned left.

The echoes of the door's closing slowly faded against distant pillars and soaring arches as the apprentices scurried along the wall. The remains of an ancient pattern of blue tiles lined the corners of the room, and Rikard stepped cautiously to avoid the slap of leather on stone that would give them away. The tiles gave out as they neared the far wall, replaced by sheets of stone laced with streaks of metal that shimmered in the glow of the brightly glowing Diviners hung from the ceiling.

Dominique stopped and tugged on Rikard's sleeve to bring his head close to hers, and pointed into the distance along the wall.

"Stairs," she whispered, and Rikard followed the direction of her finger and saw wide steps rising upward.

Rikard glanced behind, but saw no sign of the Forge's armored guardian, and so they proceeded cautiously toward the stairs, clinging to the few shadows cast by the pillars when possible.

There was no concealment on the stairs themselves, and Rikard mounted them with his shoulders hunched, stooping as low as he could against the weight of hundreds of imagined gazes, his whole body poised for flight like a deer under the hunter's draw.

They climbed slowly, following the stairs as they wound majestically around the deep well in their center, until at last the steps opened into a grand chamber. Scattered Diviners provided soft pools of light against the bases of pillars wider than a man's arms could reach, creating a long row of glowing islands across the dark sea of the chamber's floor. Squares of misty grey hung above them in the highest reaches of the vaulted ceiling, utterly baffling Rikard until he understood with a start that they must be tall windows beginning to brighten with the first dim light of dawn. More patches of light marked the entrances to wide hallways entering the far reaches of the chamber, and Rikard realized that they stood in a room of immense size.

"The Guildhall," Dominique whispered. "We're in the Guildhall."

"I'm glad you know where we are," Rikard replied quietly. "How do we get out?"

"I don't know, I'm all turned around," Dominique peered across the darkened room. "The Grandmaster's Tower is one way, the Close is another, and you must be able to get to the library from here as well, but I don't know…"

"We don't want any of that," Rikard realized. "All those entrances are watched by the Garde, all the time."

"What, then?"

"The gardens," Rikard decided. "If we can get to the terrace, we could just drop down the wall."

"Just drop down… it's taller than that." Dominique frowned. "We'll break a leg, at least."

"The gardens aren't flat. We can find a hill, or a tree or something."

"All right. Which way to the gardens?"

"That way." Rikard pointed to one of the distant hallways with certainty.

"How do you know that?" asked Dominique skeptically.

"That's east," Rikard replied smugly. "Just observe the windows."

"Ahhh," Dominique sighed, and Rikard caught a flash of her teeth in the shadows as she smiled. "Well done."

Rikard thanked the darkness as he felt heat wash across his skin, but all feelings of satisfaction fled as they began the long trek across the chamber and through the Guildhall. The vaults took every brush of leather against stone, every sigh of cloth against skin, and spitefully flung them into the shadows to echo against distant stone. The hallways were no better, as the apprentices darted from shadow to shadow along their length, pressing back behind pillars when footsteps warned them of the approach of Garde patrols. But eventually Rikard felt a cool touch of air on his sweat-streaked skin and smelled the heavy breath of damp earth, and he gratefully followed that trail through a wide archway and onto the broad terrace that lined the eastern side of the Guildhall.

Thin streaks of pink feathered the horizon beyond the black dome of the Garden Palace, but a few stars still glimmered in the thick indigo of the sky. Rikard hurried to the terrace rail and peered into the gardens. Jumbled shadows stretched beneath him, the confused tangle of the thick tree canopy. Rikard had a vague recollection of taller trees to the north, and hurried in that direction, pausing frequently to stare hopefully over the railing.

"Hurry," Dominique hissed at him, but Rikard needed no urging.

"I am," he whispered back.

Then he saw what he was hunting for, a tangle of leaves brushing against the stones just below the railing, and a thick, curved branch, too far to present a threat of anyone climbing up, but an easy drop down. *At least, not too far,* he corrected himself. *We will see about easy.*

"Here we go," Rikard tried to say confidently.

Dominique glanced at the drop, smiled, and swung her slim, brown legs over the railing without hesitation.

"I think…" Rikard began, but Dominique stepped gracefully onto the branch before he could continue and landed easily, holding on while the branch swayed and rocked under her weight.

I guess it is easy. Rikard was surprised. He waited for Dominique to disappear down the branch, hopped over the railing, and stepped confidently onto the tree limb. The bough writhed away from his feet as if it were made of smoke, and his sandals slipped from the smooth bark. Rikard clutched wildly at the branch and managed to wrap both arms around it for a moment before the weight of his body twisted him free and he plummeted toward the ground.

He landed heavily and rolled down a steep slope, coming to a rest spread-eagled as twigs and leaves rained down onto him. He had time to take a quick inventory of scrapes and bruises before Dominique landed lightly beside him, and discovered to his surprise that he had escaped any real injury.

Dominique helped him brush the worst of the dirt and leaves from his robes while mostly suppressing the small giggles that occasionally escaped her lips.

"That wasn't exactly what—" Rikard began, but he suddenly stopped. Twigs snapped and rustled as something large moved in the bushes surrounding the apprentices. Rikard caught a glimpse of a tall, steel helmet with a high plume. *The Garde!* He tensed, ready to run, although he knew it was far too late.

Dominique acted faster. She flung herself onto Rikard, wrapping her arms around his neck and pressing her lips to his. He froze in shock, overwhelmed by the heat of her lips, the warm smell of her skin, and the soft press of her breasts against his chest through the thin cloth of their robes. His arms curled around her shoulders of their own accord, an instant before the Garde soldier burst through the leaves. Dominique quickly rolled free, and the two apprentices stared at the soldier. Terror, guilt, and sublime satisfaction warred for dominance across Rikard's face, and he could only hope that the soldier would think those emotions the natural reaction to being caught in the bushes with another apprentice.

"What have we here," the soldier accosted Rikard. Before the apprentice could answer, Dominique gasped as a second soldier appeared to their right.

Rikard had not been close to any of the Garde before, except to pass by them as they stood watch beside the gates, never giving them a second glance. He had not realized how large they were. Rikard was taller than most men he encountered, but both of the soldiers were at least a handspan taller than the apprentice, and powerfully built through the shoulders and arms.

"Nothing," Rikard insisted. "We were just…"

"Were you," the soldier stated.

"Well… yes," Rikard admitted.

"The gardens are off-limits after curfew," the soldier informed Rikard gravely.

"I told you," Dominique snorted, and shoved Rikard's shoulder away from her. "Bastard."

"Oops," the second soldier told Rikard mockingly. "You should always listen to the lady."

"I know, but…" Rikard said helplessly, and he tilted his head significantly toward Dominique.

The soldier drew himself up sternly, but Rikard noticed his glance dart toward the slender form of the young woman sitting next to him.

"I'll only report you for curfew violation this time, but if I catch you out here again you'll spend the night in the Citadelle, do you understand? Now then, what are your names, and college?"

Rikard reluctantly told the soldiers. There was no help for it, as they would soon learn the truth if the apprentice had lied. Sure enough, the soldiers escorted the apprentices all the way to Killian and solemnly turned them over to the porter with a stern report.

"In the bushes, were they?" the porter asked gleefully. "Oh dear, oh dear. And what were they doing there?"

"None of your business," Dominique snapped, but the porter only tutted at them sadly and shook his head.

"Whatever will Master Quentin say?" the porter wondered. "Caught in the bushes, oh dear."

Dominique stalked to the tower, but Rikard hesitated for a moment, and whispered to the soldiers, "Thank you."

"You've got a bed. Use it next time," the soldier told him, not unkindly, and Rikard nodded gratefully and hurried after Dominique.

She waited for him just inside the tower, and Rikard closed the door behind him with a sigh of relief.

"Well done," he said quietly. "That was quick thinking."

"It felt obvious," Dominique shrugged.

It did? Rikard wondered, and he felt an ache build in his throat that made him swallow heavily. *Obvious… because she's thought of kissing me before? Or…*

"Come on." Dominique began to climb the creaky stairs. "Let's see if the others are home."

But their fellow apprentices were nowhere in the tower, and their beds appeared un-slept in. Rikard felt dread churn in his stomach, instantly banishing any feelings of comfort that had started to stir.

"What if they are still in Dorian's study, waiting for us?"

"They would have the sense to leave before the sun came up," Dominique decided. "Maybe they're hiding, waiting for classes to begin? That's what we would be doing if we hadn't been caught."

"I suppose so, but we need to go and find them as soon as we can," Rikard insisted. "And we need to return the journal to the library as well. It won't appear so innocent, now that they have caught us right under the Guildhall walls."

"We need to hurry, then. The porter won't wait long before he goes to Master Quentin to report us."

They paused only long enough to don fresh robes and wash the remaining dirt from their faces, then peered through the small window in the hall until they saw the porter scurrying toward the Master's Tower. As soon as he disappeared inside, they raced across the quad and out the gates.

"You take the journal back, I'll go and find Theirn and Clément," Dominique decided as soon as they were out of sight of Killian's walls. "We can meet back at college."

"Be safe," Rikard cautioned her.

"I will." Dominique flashed a smile and hurried away, leaving Rikard to join the trickle of bleary-eyed apprentices yawning their way toward the library.

Once inside the imposing doors, Rikard surreptitiously removed the journal from his bag. It appeared to have survived its journey intact, with only a small dent in the cover where a branch must have scored it, and a bit of a damp stain along the edge of the pages.

Rikard headed straight for the labyrinth of the cellars, but he was stopped on the verge of entering the dingy, cobweb-infested alcove in which the journal belonged by the glow of light and the sound of shuffling feet. Rikard peered around the brick archway and saw the robed figure of a master humming happily to herself as she busily sorted through the contents of the alcove's chests.

Martyr's tears, Rikard cursed silently. He could see the box he needed access to, still perched on its shelf in the back of the alcove, but there was no way to get to it without being seen, and Rikard was desperate to avoid any connection with the journal.

He crept down the cluttered hallway and lurked in a nearby room, pretending to be engrossed in the barrels of scrolls stored there while he kept an eye on the shifting light shining into the hall. Time crawled by, and still, the master did not appear. The journal felt slick in his hands, and he tucked it into his bag. A second millennium passed, then a third, until he heard the faint song of Polonius' Chronometer calling noon, and the master settled on one of the larger crates to unpack a parcel of bread and hard cheese, muttering contentedly about lunch as she did.

Rikard did not dare to wait any longer and fled the library with Aldric's journal still stowed in his bag. *I will have to bring it back later, that's all,* he decided.

His heart did not slow until he returned to the reading room. He mopped his face with his sleeve, calmed his breathing, and walked quietly out the doors and into the brilliant sunshine.

Rikard flew back to Killian college, and pushed through the door to the tower's study without a thought other than a hope that someone had made tea. But the study was empty. The three cracked leather chairs faced the small hearth, and the scarred table of engraved oak stood near the narrow, pane-glass window, but no one reclined wearily in the chairs or sat hunched over their craft at the table.

Rikard leaned into the hall and shouted, "Hello!" but the tower remained silent. He shook his head, irritated that whatever had happened, his three classmates had not waited for him.

He began to cross the study to the windows, intending to swing them open, as the room was stifling hot, but he stopped as he stepped on a sheaf of parchment strewn across the floor, his scholar's training causing him to jerk away at the first harsh crinkle of sound as if he had stepped on a glowing coal.

Rikard bent without thinking and began to scoop up the parchments, dozens of pages that had spilled from the table across the floor. Rikard recognized Clément's hasty scrawl and his striking illustrations, fortunately unharmed from the fall to the floor. He returned them to the table next to a precise line of quills, ready and sharpened, and an open pot, the ink crusted in the heat.

Rikard mopped his brow with the sleeve of his robes and glanced around the study. The room was far warmer than a spring day would warrant, and Rikard soon found the cause. The small stove had been lit and was glowing with heat, and a kettle stood on the stove's plate, long-since boiled dry. Rikard grabbed the kettle with a thick cloth and quickly hung it from its hook, for its heat was such that the cloth barely saved his fingers from blisters. Then he closed the vents on the stove and threw open the windows to clear the room.

There is something wrong here. They might have forgotten the kettle, but leaving Clément's papers strewn on the floor? And how long would the kettle have screamed before it went dry? Did no one hear it?

Rikard's thoughts were interrupted by the creak of heavy steps on the stairs. For a moment relief washed through him, and he faced the doors with an expectant smile on his face. However, when the door swung open it was not his fellow apprentices, but two of the Garde, who filled the doorway with gleaming steel armor and black capes.

"Apprentice Rikard," one of the soldiers stated.

"Yes, sir."

The soldiers entered the room, one stepping to the side while the other approached the apprentice. The tall, black plumes on their helms brushed against the thick beams of the ceiling, and Rikard could hear the floor creak as they moved.

"You're to come with us," the soldier announced as he came to a stop facing Rikard, his thumbs hooked into his belt. The soldier was older than Rikard by little more than a decade, but the apprentice suddenly felt as if he were a small child.

"Come where?" Rikard asked, profoundly relieved that his voice had come out sounding unconcerned.

"With us," the soldier answered, and he glanced at his companion, who took a step closer.

"Of course," Rikard said easily, before the soldier could take another step. "Must use the privy first, just a moment." He forced himself to walk calmly past the soldier and into the hall before the soldier could respond, and firmly shut the privy door behind him. Without hesitating, he unlatched the window and crawled through onto the steeply-pitched roof, then lowered himself cautiously to the top of the college wall. From there it was an easy drop into the alley, and Rikard was around the corner before he dared to glance back, but there was no sign of any pursuit or outcry.

Simple Frolics

Rikard hurried through the colleges, losing himself in the twists and turns of the alleys until he, at last, reached the library, where he quickly concealed himself behind a table laden with books.

I'm in trouble. They don't send the Garde to collect wayward students, it's worse than that. What do they know? Rikard peeked around the books, cautious to duck back before he made eye contact with anyone.

If they had seen us in the Guildhall last night, they would have grabbed us then. Did we leave something behind, or somehow tip them off that someone had been in the Forge? Did they find the door in the Hall of Demonstration? And that made them suspicious of the two apprentices they caught kissing in the bushes? Did they catch Theirn and Clément? We must have given ourselves away somehow, else why would they come for us today? Rikard was convinced that soldiers had visited the college before he had arrived, and taken his friends, just as they had tried to do with him. *They don't send soldiers if they just want to talk. They send a master to tell you how serious it is. No, those soldiers grabbed the others so fast they didn't have time to put a stopper on the ink pot.*

Rikard risked another peek, but the room remained gratifyingly free of soldiers.

What do I do? Leaving is risky. I'll never make it through any of the gates, and even if I did, where would I go? I don't even have my purse, and it's a long walk to Vordoux. Besides, I can't leave if the others are in trouble, too. I have to help them, somehow.

Rikard's mind spun in circles, the same questions orbiting endlessly without ever finding clarity. *What do they know? What do I do?*

He groaned in frustration and slowly pounded his forehead on the table, hoping to jar something loose within his befuddled brain, but it did no good. *I need help,* was the best it could come up with. But that thought did bring with it a course of action, even if it was far from being a real plan.

Fine. So what do I do while I wait? Rikard realized the library was as good a hiding place as he could think of. Dozens of other apprentices, all with their noses buried in their books, provided excellent cover. *Write everything down,* he decided. *Make sure nothing is lost.*

A quick trip to an unattended table netted him a quill and a scroll of blank parchment, and he scribbled tiny notes to himself while steadfastly refusing to glance at the quill's perplexed owner when she returned to her table.

His parchment slowly filled as the sun's rays marched across the floor and ascended one of the walls, and it was practically full when the hall suddenly dimmed as the light finally fled. Rikard painstakingly blew the last of the ink dry and tied the parchment into a roll as several apprentices empowered the chandeliers, their Words a soft rhythm that beat against his chest like distant thunder on a hot evening.

The Chronometer chimed evening bells as Rikard left the library and slowly made his way through the gardens, sticking to the winding paths that burrowed deepest through the flower-laden bushes, always ready to step off the trail and into the shrubberies should any of the Garde appear.

The sun finally sank into a golden haze behind the low hills that marched to the horizon west of Criénne, and the sky became an indigo so thick that the first stars appeared to nestle in it as if they rested on a quilted pillow. Rikard waited until those first daring arrivals had been joined by a thick stream of companions, a gossamer web of light that brushed the dark silhouette of the Forge tower, and the yellow glow of lanterns had been kindled in the windows of the colleges as if in warm imitation of the cold sparkles above.

Then he retraced his steps to Killian college.

The porter had returned to his post at the gate, sitting comfortably in a small pool of light in his lodge as his finger slowly traced lines of text in a small, parchment-wrapped book. Rikard left him to his read, not daring to try and slip past. All new students learned in their first week that the college porters were chosen for their preternatural sense of hearing, usually much to the amusement of the older apprentices.

Instead, Rikard availed himself of the kitchen gate with the latch that came free of its hook as soon as the gate was lifted even slightly, then crept through the deserted passageways to the coal bins that filled the small yard behind the dining hall. Rikard doubted that anyone would be coming for coal until the apprentices began their morning chores, so he settled with his back against the rough bricks of the wall and waited to see the warm glow of a lantern in a particular window of the wide tower that housed the masters' lodgings.

It was much later than he had expected before he saw the light. Most of the rest of the college was dark, and the night air had turned cool enough that Rikard had wrapped his arms tightly around himself for warmth, his thin robes no match for the chill.

It was a quick walk along the colonnade to the Master's Tower, and Rikard forced himself to stride with his head up, trusting the shadows to disguise him as any other apprentice, hurrying to his master's call.

He tapped lightly on the heavy wooden door, then tapped again when there was no response. A third tap finally summoned the reluctant shuffle of feet on the other side, and the door creaked open to reveal Master Quentin's face.

"Rikard? What are you doing here? What time is it?"

"It's late, Master Quentin, I'm sorry, but I didn't want to come earlier."

"Why ever not?"

"I think something has happened to the others. To Dominique, and to Clément and Theirn as well."

"Are they hurt? Rikard, what has happened to them?" Quentin ushered his apprentice into his lodgings and offered a glass of wine

"I don't know, Master Quentin. I was in the library all morning, and when I returned to college they weren't there."

"But that is not mysterious, is it? Why do you think something has happened to them?"

"There had been a struggle. I know that sounds ridiculous, Master Quentin, but I am sure of it. Clément's papers were all over the floor, and the kettle had boiled completely dry."

"A kettle and some papers are hardly sinister. Did you tell anyone?"

"No, Master Quentin. Before I could, the Garde came, and they didn't care about anything but telling me that I had to come with them. So I asked if I could use the privy, and snuck out through the window."

"You snuck out the privy window?"

"Yes, Master Quentin. It's how we get past the porter."

"Ah, I remember," Quentin replied, and he began to pace the length of his study while he collected his thoughts. Despite the late hour, the master's short steps were quick, his turns precise, as if he lectured to an attentive audience rather than an internal chorus. Quentin's hands were steepled together as if in relaxed repose, but Rikard saw that the master's fingers drummed against each other, lightly tapping out the rhythm of his ruminations, and his mouth was set in a stern line that betrayed the intensity of his thoughts.

Rikard quietly sipped from his glass as he waited, then instantly regretted it as the wine burned in his empty stomach. *Getting drunk and puking on Master Quentin's rug would certainly crown today off appropriately,* Rikard considered, and he placed the glass firmly on one of the small end tables that lurked throughout the room. *Should I tell him more? Should I tell him what we found in the journal, or about the Forge? No, it can't help. If I did it would make him part of it, and he would either have to lie to the grandmaster or turn me in.*

Quentin finally stopped his pacing and faced Rikard.

"I shall go and speak with Grandmaster Dorian about this." There was no hesitation in the master's voice, and Rikard felt a wash of relief pass through him. "If what you say is, in fact, the case, it is unforgivable. Sending the Garde into the colleges to arrest apprentices! What can he be thinking?" Quentin straightened his robes, took a resolute breath, and hurried to the door.

Rikard hesitated, unsure of how to suggest that he should stay behind without revealing more than he wished, but Quentin mistook his intent and stopped him with a raised finger.

"I believe it might be unwise for you to accompany me. At least until I have had a chance to talk to the grandmaster about this." The master's voice was kind, but his face was stern as Quentin examined Rikard, and the apprentice swallowed the lump of shame that had lodged in his throat at his deception. "You may wait here, if you wish. There is a Veil in my study that might interest you."

Quentin shut the door firmly behind him, and Rikard sank into a chair and closed his eyes, suddenly too weary to stand. *My legs are actually wobbling,* he noticed, amazed. He glanced longingly at the glass of wine, but regretfully confirmed his earlier decision and left it untouched, closed his eyes, and let his mind drift.

***

Rikard was not at all sure how long he had dozed in the chair, only that when he finally awoke he felt refreshed, and suspected that it had been some time. He stood and stretched the heaviness from his shoulders, resolutely ignored the glass of wine again, and found his way into Master Quentin's study. The comfortable room was as neat and tidy as the master himself, with his tools meticulously arranged in their boxes of polished wood and steel, and his books assembled on their shelves in ranks as rigid as any the Garde could muster. The Veil the master had mentioned was laid out on the desk on a square of soft leather. Its shell had been opened and set aside, and a small lancet lay beside it where Quentin must have set it upon hearing Rikard's knock.

Rikard stooped over the desk, not daring to sit in the master's chair, and tried to discern the Device's function, but his thoughts slipped from the intricate structures as if they were water through a grate, returning over and over to endless speculation on what might be taking place inside the imposing tower of the grandmasters.

He soon gave up on the Veil and wandered to the shelves, but the dark spines of the books did no more than the Device to distract him, and he found himself re-reading the gilded letters over and over without any notion of what words they formed.

Shortly after Rikard had decided that Quentin was not returning, but before the apprentice could decide where he should go next, the harsh click of the door latch in the main room made him jump. Master Quentin's quick tread crossed the room and the man himself appeared in the doorway, his round face flushed and his grey hair wafting in strange, never-before-seen disarray.

"Rikard, good, you are still here," the master panted, and paused to mop his brow with the sleeve of his robe.

"Are you well, Master Quentin?" Rikard hurried to lead the master to a chair, but Quentin waved off his apprentice.

"I am fine, just winded. I ran all the way from the gardens!"

Rikard felt a vice clamp around his throat at the master's words, and he swallowed heavily. *That doesn't sound good.* "Did you speak with Grandmaster Dorian?"

"I did, and I fear that the situation may be far worse than you imagined." Quentin dabbed his brow again and glared at the wet patch on his sleeve. "Dorian was most unhappy when I asked him if he knew where my missing apprentices were. Pleaded ignorance until I told him that they had been seen being led away by the Garde, at which point he demanded to know who had told me."

"Did you…?" Rikard held his breath.

"I mentioned that there were several masters in college this morning who had seen the soldiers. A feeble tale, but one that was hard to immediately disprove. In any case, it served its purpose, as Grandmaster Dorian told me, in no uncertain terms, that your fellow apprentices were indeed inside the Citadelle, and that I should rest assured that he would 'deal with them tomorrow.' "

"What does that mean?"

"I am not certain, but the grandmaster was furious. He wished to know if I had seen you, and when I protested at the treatment of the others, he suggested that I should forget about them, and concentrate on serving the Guild better. It did not seem an idle threat."

"What did you say, Master Quentin?" Rikard held his breath. *He's known me less than a year, and the Guild is his life.*

"I said, 'yes, sir!' and ran out of there as fast as I could," Quentin shook his head, "although I did not actually start running until I reached the gardens, as I have explained. Speaking of which, will you make us some tea, Rikard? I am quite parched."

Rikard hurried to obey, carefully filling the silver tea ball with leaves while the ancient kettle creaked and hissed on the stove. Rikard wondered if the sun would rise before the kettle boiled, as the stove's fire had dwindled to just a few ashen coals, but finally, the dented spout gave off a feeble sigh that counted as boiling as far as Rikard was concerned.

Rikard carried teapot and cup to the study, where he found Quentin immersed in a book freshly removed from its home, judging from the gap on the shelf next to him.

"Ahhh, thank you, Rikard," Quentin murmured as he accepted the cup and took a sip. "Perhaps let the kettle boil next time, as it does wonders for the strength. Never mind." Quentin waved aside Rikard's apologies and pointed the apprentice to the high-backed chair in front of the master's desk. "Now, will you please explain to me what you and the others have been up to?"

"Master Quentin, I'm not sure—"

"Apprentice Rikard, I am not so feeble-minded that I can no longer read between the lines, as it were. Grandmaster Dorian does not quietly throw apprentices into the Citadelle for simple frolics. In fact, he revels in making an example of them. Nor does he lie to his masters about such a thing. Now, if you wish for my help, you will kindly tell me what it is that you have done."

Rikard gulped. "Yes, Master Quentin. We were curious, after Aldric's Gaze, when Grandmaster Dorian told us off."

"Of course you were," Quentin sighed, sipped from his cup, and sadly placed it on his desk. "Continue, please."

"We decided to see what we could find in the library. Dominique, Theirn, and I, anyway. Then we snuck into Grandmaster Dorian's study, to read the books he had there."

"I see. And what did you find?" Quentin's eyes narrowed suspiciously. "Or is there more?"

Rikard nodded miserably. *It seems so stupid, now. What were we thinking?* "Yes, Master Quentin. I had found a journal in the library, that told of a passageway between the grandmaster's study and the archives. So we opened it. But we got lost and couldn't find a way out for ages, and when we did, it wasn't the archives. It was the Forge."

"You went to the Forge?" Quentin's eyes widened in shock. "But, Rikard, that is grounds for arrest on its own, or worse! No one may enter the Forge who is not a grandmaster. Why would you go to the Forge? Why do any of this?"

"It's all in here." Rikard passed Quentin the scroll containing his notes, hastily scrawled in the library that afternoon. "Everything."

Quentin unrolled the parchment, squinted at Rikard's tiny scribbles, carefully unfolded his spectacles, and perched them on his nose.

"Why Rikard, if only you had demonstrated such dedication in your previous studies," Quentin observed as he peered at the parchment.

"Yes, Master Quentin."

Quentin returned to his reading and Rikard remained silent, gazing at his clenched fingers as he wondered if he had made the right decision to reveal their transgressions to the master. *What other choice was there?* he thought miserably. Quentin appeared to be taking the scroll seriously, at least. The master read with a frown of concentration on his face and frequently paused to return to a previous passage. Several times he rose from his chair and took down a book from the study's shelves, carefully turning the thick pages until he found the passage he was seeking, then returned to the scroll. At last Quentin reached the end of the scroll and remained standing near the shelves, stroking his chin, his gaze lost amongst the spines of his books.

"I have never heard of this man, Lazarre, whom you claim was the founder of the Guild," Quentin said quietly. "If, as you say, he proceeded to also found the Crunorix, that is not surprising. However, it is well-known that many of the grandmasters were lost in the war against the Nameless King. Eleven, if I remember my histories."

"Eleven? Master Quentin, that is the same number that Aldric wrote joined with Lazarre. Do you not think that is significant? If Aldric was trying to cover up—"

"Yes, Rikard, that is why I mentioned it."

"Sorry, Master Quentin.

"That is quite all right. As I was saying, I have not heard of Lazarre before, nor any of these other things that you say Aldric's journal mentions. Vessel, Guardian… never. Only the Source is familiar, of course. Your notes make for grim reading."

"Yes, sir. We thought the same."

"You have the journal?"

"I do, Master Quentin. I wanted to take it back, but there wasn't the chance."

"A terrible risk, to keep it, but perhaps a fortunate one. I will need to examine it myself, you understand, to see if I reach the same conclusions as you did as to its author and reliability, but that will have to wait until tomorrow."

"Yes, Master Quentin. If you do agree with us… if you think the journal is really Grandmaster Aldric's…"

"Well, it is certainly a fascinating revelation. A black secret in the heart of the Guild's history. I shall be interested to see if Grandmaster Dorian knew of this already. However, I am not sure why any of this drove you into such flagrant disobedience. If

I am to help you, I must be able to explain that there were extenuating circumstances, that you were acting to the benefit of the Guild, with the Guild's best interests at heart."

"Yes, sir, we were," Rikard assured the master. "Much of what Aldric wrote seemed to reference the Gaze. It was on the same page in the journal. And as the Gaze was suddenly active, we thought, isn't it possible, that everything Aldric was saying, that it wasn't ancient history at all? That it was happening again, right now?"

"You concluded that the Gaze was somehow linked to the origins of the Guild, and its ties with the Crunorix?"

"Yes, Master Quentin. We hoped to find proof of that, but we didn't find anything. I still don't understand why Grandmaster Dorian was so upset that we saw Aldric's Gaze light up. None of this explains that."

"Ahhh, well, I believe I might be able to help there. As it was told to me by Grandmaster Dorian, Aldric's Gaze was created with one specific purpose, to watch for the empowering of an apostate forge."

"An apostate... forge? Is that possible?"

"In theory, someone could create the Device. Aldric created one, or, I suppose, if we are to believe what you have uncovered, Lazarre did, so why could not someone else? But to envision an apostate of such skill being able to conceal himself, let alone replicating Lazarre's work in secret, not to mention the singular nature of the Source itself... well, it has never happened. Nevertheless, one can understand the concern, and therefore the extreme... reaction... that Grandmaster Dorian evinced."

"Yes, Master Quentin, I do see that, but what does an apostate forge have to do with Lazarre or the Crunorix?"

"I cannot think how it would, except for a theory that came to me as I read your notes, just now. An extremely tenuous theory, really no more than supposition. It shames me to voice it.

"It intrigues me that your notes say that Lazarre split the Source 'in half'. I mentioned a moment ago that insurmountable obstacle facing the creation of an apostate forge, the Source, unique in all the world, irreplaceable, inimitable. With that in mind… well, what conclusion do your thoughts reach?"

"If Lazarre split the Source, then he could have created his own forge, a Crunorix forge, and that's what Aldric's Gaze is watching for."

"Exactly. As I said, extremely tenuous."

"No, Master Quentin, that has to be it."

"No, it does not. There are probably many other explanations that could fit the tale, including the most likely, that the story of Lazarre is untrue. However, it is intriguing, is it not?"

"What about the Vessel? Aldric said that Lazarre tore the Source from the Vessel before he split it, and then Aldric says that the Vessel was killed in the war and that the Source was lost. Grandmaster Aldric calls the Vessel 'she,' Master Quentin."

"I saw that in your notes. Fanciful language to refer to some form of Device that contained the Source, I imagine, much as sailors refer to their vessels as 'she'."

"And the part about the Source being lost?"

"Well, that is clearly mere fantasy. The Source is in the Forge, and has been for one thousand years. The rest of what you found, that is what piques my interest."

"But, if it is true, then what does it mean that Aldric's Gaze found what it was searching for? Are the Crunorix back?"

"I would hardly think so," Quentin laughed. "Far more likely is that someone has found the secret forge. Perhaps an apostate, exactly as Dorian explained."

"Then, this has nothing to do with the Crunorix at all?"

"You sound disheartened. No, I do not think that is likely."

"Just a waste of time. All we did was get ourselves into trouble. We thought we had uncovered something, I don't know… sinister. Instead, all Dorian is doing is trying to keep it secret that there's an apostate out there with a forge."

"I suspect that is correct, although…" Quentin let the parchment dangle from his fingers, forgotten, as he stared across the room, his gaze unfocused. Rikard managed to stifle his impatience, desperate to know what had triggered the master's introspection.

"There are two pieces of information in your research that may speak to something more." Quentin frowned and thoughtfully examined the parchment again. "Here, where you noted the tirade of Grandmaster Évarice in the Assembly against this man Duibhir."

"Who is Duibhir, Master Quentin?"

"I believe him to be the same Duibhir who was one of Ruric's knights, called the 'Hooded Knight' by some."

"I haven't heard of him, Master Quentin."

"Few have, I suppose, but he was at the Conclave, and I believe he became the first leader of the Gravewardens, so he was a man of consequence, for all that history has forgotten him. A Gravewarden tower is, perhaps, what Évarice was referring to."

"And the other things that Évarice mentions? The Guardian that Duibhir has hidden?"

"Unfortunately, I have no idea, but it is clearly significant to Évarice and in some way germane to the Gaze. I cannot rationalize why the Gravewardens would have any concern with an apostate forge, or hiding a Guardian of such a forge, and that gives me pause, for if the Gravewardens are involved, it suggests a link with the Crunorix in some way that is not clear to me.

"Interestingly, the reason we remember Duibhir today, those of us who do remember him, is for his scrolls. He wrote extensively of the Conclave and the events surrounding the great war."

"That's it, then," Rikard said excitedly. "We need to read those scrolls and see if he mentions a Guardian or the Gaze."

"You are not alone in wishing you could read the scrolls. They were kept in the archives of Fellgate Castle and were lost in the Cataclysm. Scholars have attempted to track down transcriptions and copies for centuries."

"A copy, then," Rikard suggested. "Where can we find a copy?"

"I have no idea. I am hardly an historian, Rikard. But perhaps we could ask those who are. The Temple archives are likely the best source. I can send a message to their Archivist in

Bandirma, a man named Whitebrooke, I believe, but it will be many weeks or even months before we might hear a reply."

"You said two things, Master Quentin."

"Ahhh, yes. Is not the second one obvious? You have seen the Forge, Rikard. One note in your description stands out to me above all others. What strikes you about what you saw, that might make the revelation of a second Forge even more significant?"

"The Forge is nearly empty, Master Quentin."

"The Forge is nearly empty," Quentin agreed. "The Source is nearly consumed, a secret that Dorian has revealed to no one. The end of the Guild, perhaps in your lifetime. Now, if Lazarre really did split the Source, and created a second forge…"

"A new supply, Master Quentin. A new life for the Guild."

"Exactly."

"You think it's true. Everything about Lazarre."

"Yes, I do. It explains how there could possibly be another forge when it would otherwise seem impossible. The Source cannot be replicated, and no apostate could have the skill to create the Device itself, yet Aldric's Gaze tells us that such a forge does indeed exist. The story of Lazarre provides the explanation. So far, it is only supposition, but I would wager we can track down the proof, given enough time in the archives."

"Doesn't that seem a bit… risky? And how would it help us with Dominique and the others?"

"Quite right." The master shook his head slightly and smiled apologetically. "We must decide what to do tonight. I fear that we have fallen under the thrall of academic pursuits when we should instead be considering more urgent matters."

"Yes, Master Quentin. Now that we know Dominique, Clément, and Theirn are in the Citadelle, we can assess how best to get them out. We can't just leave them there."

Quentin examined Rikard's face in silence for a moment as the master's smile grew. "You astonish me, my boy. I only thought to ensure your passage from the Guild until I could call for an Assembly to sort all this out. But of course, you are absolutely right. The fate of your classmates lurked in the back of my mind, and I must say I would be very pleased to have your help. Are you certain, Rikard? No one would think less of you if you chose to let the masters sort out this mess."

"No, Master Quentin," Rikard smiled apologetically, "but I know I would think less of myself if I didn't help."

"Well done," Quentin beamed. "However, you have now revealed my utter lack of a plan, other than to order the Garde to release them into my custody and trust that my word is enough."

"Do you think that will work?" Rikard asked, unable to keep incredulity from creeping into his voice.

"It might," Quentin protested, but then instantly relented with a shrug. "If it does not, I will demand their presence at the Assembly, to testify, and we can show the masters that you acted in the best interests of the Guild."

"Yes, Master Quentin." Rikard swallowed heavily as he considered the churn of unease in his stomach. "But, what if they are never allowed to speak at the Assembly? It would be my word against the grandmaster's, in the end, even if you convince the other masters to listen. What if Dorian does not allow an Assembly?"

"Not allow an Assembly?" Quentin shook his head, befuddled. "I have never heard of such a thing."

"Very well, Master Quentin," Rikard allowed, "but there's no telling what will happen to Dominique, Theirn, and Clément in the Citadelle, or if they'll be allowed to speak at an Assembly about what we've found. We must get them out."

"Hmmm, I do not share your pessimism, Rikard, but I agree it is best to be certain they speak at the Assembly, and it was a dirty business to lock them up in the Citadelle, in the first place. So, we will hope the Garde turns them over to me when I ask."

The master began to re-assemble the case of the Device on his workbench, his nimble fingers quickly securing the intricate layers of metal within its polished wooden shell. He held up the finished product for inspection, a globe of interlocking pieces surrounded by bands of silver. "If they do not, then this will certainly come in handy."

A Wet, Red Stain

The Citadelle crouched above the River Gates, a ziggurat of red stone with none of the graceful, pillar-lined balconies that adorned the Guild halls. The Citadelle's walls were featureless save for protruding guard towers at regular intervals, pierced with narrow windows that glared across the river at the sprawling city of Criénne. Even in the middle of the night, the walls of the Citadelle were lit with dozens of glowing Diviners, making the walls seem to throb as if they were but recently removed from the kiln.

Despite his long legs, Rikard had to hurry to keep pace with Master Quentin, who showed no signs of his recent dash across the gardens. Nor did they attempt any concealment, hurrying across echoing courtyards and along empty corridors at such a speed that it felt to Rikard that mere moments had passed before the thick gates of the Citadelle appeared before him.

Quentin resolutely ignored the two Garde soldiers standing watch outside the gates and plunged through the postern without hesitation.

But once inside, the master halted and quietly took his bearings. Heavy stone pillars marched across a polished floor to a wide staircase that led up to the second floor, but after a moment,

Quentin decided on a small door that led to a featureless, narrow passageway instead.

"Do you know where we are going?" Rikard whispered.

"I have been here once before," Quentin replied absently, distracted as he peered down an equally barren hallway that crossed their own. "I believe this will take us through the barracks, and then we must find some stairs."

"The barracks? Master Quentin, aren't the barracks going to be full of soldiers?"

"Sleeping soldiers," Quentin pointed out. "It's the ones who are awake that we want to avoid. In any case, we won't be going into their dormitories."

"Yes, Master Quentin, but do you not think they might have guards? It is a fortress," Rikard reminded him reasonably.

"Perhaps," allowed Quentin. "You clearly have a suggestion, Rikard, out with it. A rescue is no time to stand on ceremony, after all."

"No, sir," Rikard agreed with a grin. "Well, the two soldiers out front didn't bat an eye when we passed them, and as you said, perhaps your word as a master is enough."

"Are you suggesting we announce ourselves to the guards?"

"Why not? I did it all the time back in Vordoux. You can get all sorts of things with a smile and the right accent. Once, we convinced–"

"I do understand," Quentin interrupted. "This is hardly boyhood larks, Rikard, and these soldiers are not some foolish tavern-keeper."

"No, sir," Rikard grinned sheepishly. "And it was the daughters of Comte Léopold. Not a tavern-keeper."

"Was it indeed? A tale for another time, I think. I believe we are unlikely to encounter the young Comtesses tonight, yet you may have a point."

They retraced their steps to the entrance hall and ascended the stairs, soon encountering a group of Garde soldiers standing vigilantly beside the wide archway that led to the interior of the Citadelle. Quentin approached them confidently, a stern frown affixed on his face.

"Will one of you tell us where the cells are?"

"I'm sorry, sir, but no one is allowed down there without an escort," one of the soldiers replied.

"Then please take us there. Right away."

"I'm sorry, sir," the guard repeated. "We can't leave our post."

"Summon someone who can take us, and be quick about it." Quentin produced the small Device from his robes and examined it. "We do not have much time," he added ominously.

The soldier hurried to obey and soon returned with another soldier to guide Quentin and Rikard through the Citadelle. They followed through twisting hallways and down stairs until Rikard had little idea of where they were. *We would never have found the cells on our own,* he realized. *Not for days.*

Their guide certainly knew where they were going, and they were soon following him along a low passageway, far underground. Heavy blocks of granite lined the floor and walls, and thick pillars supported the low ceiling, unadorned save for the chiseled scars of the stone's shaping. A few lanterns provided small islands of light along the passage, but between them Rikard was forced to trust the builders to have provided a level floor, for the shadows were so thick, there could have been a gaping hole under every step, and he would never have known until the fateful plunge began.

At long last they reached the end of the passage and a heavy iron door recessed into the wall. Their guide rapped on the door, his gauntleted hand producing a heavy, flat echo. A small window in the door slid open and they were examined by dark eyes for a moment before the window snapped shut and the sound of heavy gears clanking deep within the door filled the hallway. Rikard counted four distinct clunks as whatever mechanism fastening the door withdrew, then the door slowly swung open.

They stepped into a wide room dominated by a long table in the center of the floor. Wooden racks holding spears and shields stood against the walls, and a second door, twin to the one they had just passed through, stood open directly across the room.

Rikard counted four soldiers seated at the table playing dice, then upped the count to five as another entered the room through a smaller, wooden door the apprentice had not noticed, buckling his sword belt back in place as he did. Two more soldiers sat near the weapon rack, cleaning their blades and polishing their armor, and a final two joined the soldier who had opened the door, standing with their hands resting casually on their sword hilts in a posture so identical to the one adopted by the soldiers who had visited Rikard in his study that for a moment he feared that these were, in fact, the same men.

"Good evening, Master," one of the soldiers greeted them. The soldier's wide jaw and high cheekbones appeared to have been carved from the same granite as the walls, and the dark skin of his shaved head gleamed in the light of the lanterns. The soldier spoke Venaissine with the short, clipped vowels of the Summer Coast, but Rikard had no trouble understanding the wary caution in his tone. "What can we do for you?"

"I need to take the prisoners. Right away," Quentin replied, and Rikard was amazed at the master's assured tone. "Where are they?" Quentin demanded, glancing about the room as if surprised that the prisoners were not awaiting his convenience.

"Of course, Master. Their pass," he ordered the soldier who had guided them from the entrance hall, and he held out a hand expectantly.

The soldier turned pale and stood rigidly still. "I don't have their pass, Sergent."

"Why not, soldier?"

"I think the guards at the entrance hall must have asked them for it, Sergent."

"Return to your post, soldier, and report to me tomorrow for discipline."

"Yes, Sergent," the soldier replied, and fled into the passageway.

The sergent watched him go, then faced Master Quentin. "Do you have your pass, Master?"

Rikard felt his knees sag and his heart pounded in his ears. *We're caught.* He knew it, as certain as he had ever been about anything. He could not remember what he had imagined breaking into the Citadelle would be like, but it was far from the cold reality of the terrifying, invulnerable authority of the sergent standing in front of him.

"Pass? Really, Sergent, we were sent here by Grandmaster Dorian himself. It is urgent we examine the prisoners with this Diviner," Quentin spluttered, showing the sergent the small, wooden Device, but his voice sounded shrill to Rikard's ears, and the sergent appeared unimpressed.

"Only those with a pass signed by the captain or Grandmaster Dorian are allowed in." The sergent held out his hand to Quentin. "But since the grandmaster sent you, I am sure you have one, correct?"

"Of course," Quentin replied, and he began to pat the pockets of his robe, searching for the mythical parchment. "I have it right here…" he muttered, clumsy as he shifted the Device from one hand to the other. "Hold this a moment," he said absently, placing the Device in the sergent's outstretched hand. The soldier took it instinctively, and Quentin turned to Rikard, caught his gaze, and screwed his eyes shut.

Rikard understood barely in time. The master's Word pulsed through Rikard as he desperately closed his own eyes, slamming his hands over his face as brilliant light flashed blood red through his eyelids. A strange thrumming noise twisted through the room as more light throbbed warmly through the cracks in his fingers.

Rikard felt Quentin alter the Word, and the light and sound ceased, leaving behind a silence so still that Rikard could hear his heart hammering in his ears.

"It worked!" Quentin shouted in joy, and Rikard dared to open his eyes. Quentin stood in the center of the room, shaking his head in wonder as he gazed around at the soldiers. All ten stood or sat in the same positions that Rikard had last seen them in, but all had slumped as if they no longer had the will to hold themselves so rigidly upright. All wore the same expression of somewhat befuddled happiness, as if they had been given good tidings in a foreign tongue.

Quentin exhaled noisily and retrieved the small Veil from the sergent's unresisting hand. "I don't mind saying I was terrified," the master admitted. "I've never tried that on more than one person at a time, and I am not the most skilled adept, as you know."

"It worked brilliantly, Master Quentin," Rikard assured him.

"Yes, it did, didn't it?" Quentin beamed. "Now, we should try to find the others before someone else comes by."

The open door on the far side of the room led to a short passageway lined with heavy, iron bars on both sides. The space beyond the bars had been divided by thick stone walls into small cells, and here Rikard found Dominique, Clément, and Theirn, all pressed against the bars to discover the cause of the commotion from the outer room.

"Master Quentin! Thank the Maker," Theirn greeted them, and Rikard felt an uncontrollable smile spread across his face as he clasped their hands through the bars.

"The sergent has the keys," Dominique urged them, and Rikard raced to the guardroom to find them. A steel ring with a dozen keys hung from the sergent's belt, but Rikard hesitated, unable to touch them for fear of waking the soldier. He waved his hand in front of the sergent's face, and gently prodded his cheek, ready to leap away at the first sign of a response, but the sergent stood quietly, uncaring.

Rikard unhooked the keys from the soldier's belt, then stopped again, his eyes locked on the soldier's sword. It was a magnificent blade, as long as Rikard's arm, with a hilt of polished steel and a grip covered in leather dyed a rich black. Rikard glanced at the sergent's face one more time, then timidly slipped the sword free. The blade shone brightly in the lantern's light, its tapered edge curving like a leaf to a point. Rikard hefted it, feeling its balance. He had never held anything more deadly than dull practice swords, and he was shocked at how light the sergent's sword was, how quickly it responded to his motions, as if he held a piece of sunlight in his hand.

"Rikard, have you found them?" Quentin's voice carried into the guardroom.

"Yes, Master Quentin!"

Rikard slipped the sword belt from the sergent's waist and hung it over his shoulder, then hurried to the cells. He fumbled through the keys until he found the right one and threw open the doors with a dramatic flourish. Theirn thumped him enthusiastically on the shoulder, and Clément pulled him into a bear hug, so Rikard had high hopes by the time he opened the door to Dominique's cell.

"Don't cut your nose off." She smiled at him, pointing to the sword slung under his arm, and joined the others.

I deserved that for trying to play the hero, he admonished himself, a wry grin twitching at the corner of his mouth.

"Now, listen to me," Quentin instructed the apprentices, and they gathered around him in an orderly circle. Quentin smiled fondly at the ring of attentive faces and reached to grasp each one of them firmly by the shoulder as he spoke. "The hardest part is behind us now, but we are still in terrible danger. I had hoped to keep you safely at college until I could call for an Assembly, but after the events that have taken place here in the Citadelle, it is clear that Dorian will not tolerate that. You must flee the Guild, immediately, but do not despair. I promise you that I will find a way for you all to return."

"Thank you, Master Quentin," Rikard said softly, and the others echoed him in subdued voices. But Rikard could see that there was hope in their eyes, despite the task ahead of them.

"How will we escape?" Dominique asked.

"Of course, Dominique. 'How' indeed," Quentin laughed. He turned and led the group from the cells and across the guardroom. "We must make our way out of the Citadelle, of course, but you must not stop until you are far from Criénne, far from Venaissin, as far from the Guild as possible. I imagined that you would go to the docks and see if there was a boat heading for the Inner Sea, or perhaps beyond, that you could—"

"Halt!" The shout slapped Rikard in the face, and he started, shocked. Gleaming silver metal and black plumes filled the small passageway, and deafening voices demanded that they lay down their weapons, lay on the floor, surrender.

"No!" Dominique cried desperately, and Rikard saw Clément drop to his knees, his eyes wide with fear.

"Wait! Wait!" Master Quentin shouted, stepping forward with arms outstretched. "I have a pass from Grandmaster Dorian!"

Rikard saw the master reach into his pocket and draw forth the Veil. Quentin closed his eyes and began his Word.

Something made the noise of an axe striking rotten wood, and Quentin staggered back, a thick, black shaft buried in his chest. He fell to one knee, his mouth still trying to form the Word, but no sound came.

"No!" Rikard shouted, and leapt to Quentin's side, clutching at the master as Quentin slid to the ground, a wet, red stain soaking his white robes. Dominique screamed somewhere far behind him, and Rikard heard the lethal rip of something passing close to his head, then he felt his robes twitch as they were tugged over his ribs. Someone fell heavily onto Rikard's back and rolled to the side, and Rikard stared, bewildered, into Theirn's face as the apprentice lay gasping on the stone floor, a shaft buried in the ruin of his neck.

Rikard staggered to his feet. Another bolt struck the wall next to him, sending shards of stone into his cheek, and he stumbled as he kicked something on the floor. Hands grabbed at him, urging him into motion.

"Run!" Dominique shouted in his ear. Rikard grabbed Clément's shoulder, but the apprentice screamed at him and wrenched free, and threw himself to the ground. Rikard saw the object he had kicked roll to a stop against the wall behind Clément. *The Veil,* a faraway voice said in his mind, and he stooped to collect it.

"Rikard, damn it, run!" Dominique shouted again, and Rikard obeyed, forcing his legs into motion as he chased Dominique down the passage. Heavy boots pounded in the hallway behind them, but no more bolts ripped through the air, as the crossbowmen held fire for fear of hitting their comrades.

The two apprentices dashed through the pools of light and darkness, their sandals slapping heavily on the stones.

Dominique's blonde hair flashed in the light, then turned to black silhouette as she plunged into the next patch of shadow.

"Up!" she shouted as they reached a narrow staircase set in the wall, and he bounded after her. They reached a landing, but there were soldiers there, shouting and grabbing through the doorway. Rikard slammed the door and raced after Dominique, leaving behind cries of rage and pain. They passed another landing, and then another, each one leading out only onto lanterns, silver steel, and black capes, and the apprentices fled ever upward. The stairs felt endless, and Rikard felt his lungs burn as he desperately sucked air into them, but Dominique did not slow, and Rikard would not fall behind.

At last, they reached a door that opened onto an empty hallway, and they hurried along its quiet, echoing length. At the far end, a wide doorway led into blackness, and they reached its welcoming shadow before the door opened behind them to disgorge their hunters.

The apprentices found themselves on a wide parapet above the River Gate. Dominique rushed to the edge and peered over, standing on her toes to lean out as far as possible.

"We're over the river," she panted, trying to catch her breath. "We can jump."

Rikard leaned out and peered down. Far below he could make out the tiny ripples of red that marked the surface of the river, reflecting the walls of the Citadelle. A small black shape tied to the pier, no larger than his outstretched hand, was probably a barge or ferry of some kind, and Rikard felt a cold hand of despair clutch at his heart as he realized how distant they were.

"We're too high to jump," he groaned.

"But Master Quentin said to get to the docks," Dominique objected, and she pointed across the river to where the lanterns of the dock's watchmen were clearly visible, slowly moving back and forth along the pier. "They're right there," she insisted, desperation creeping into the edges of her voice.

"I know, but we have to go another way," Rikard pleaded. "Come on."

They began to run along the parapet, but before they had taken a dozen strides, lanterns swarmed onto the wall ahead of them and began to move closer, bobbing and weaving as if they were marionettes on a string.

"Shit," Rikard hissed between his teeth, and they raced back the way they had come. But the long hallway was already filled with the thunder of heavy boots and shouts of command, and the apprentices staggered to a stop again, twisting back and forth between the closing jaws of defeat.

Rikard hurried to the wall and glanced down. *At least we're not still over the pier.*

"All right, we jump," he muttered.

"And the fall?"

"Try to land on your feet," Rikard instructed, remembering the pain of days spent leaping from the cliffs near Vordoux. "Keep your legs together, cover your face, and keep your teeth clamped shut."

Dominique nodded, her eyes bright with fear, but she grabbed his hand and led him to the back of the parapet without hesitation.

"Ready?" she asked. Rikard tucked the Veil into his robes and pulled the sword belt tight around his chest. Then he nodded.

They sprinted for the outer wall, hands clenched together. They hit the top of the wall in a great bound and leapt into space, their legs and arms windmilling frantically as they fought to stay upright. They fell forever, far longer than any jump Rikard had made from the cliffs at home, until he wondered if the darkness had tricked him and there was no water beneath them, only endless night. Then suddenly the river leapt at him, and he braced his legs and clutched her hand.

He struck the water with a crack of thunder that drove through his legs and into his chest with the force of a thousand hammers. Then a hammer struck him under the jaw, and there was only darkness.

The Apostate

Rikard awoke to the creak of wood and the soft gurgle of water. His face and jaw throbbed hideously, a bottomless agony that sent fingers of fire into his shoulders and chest. He groaned and instantly regretted it, as fresh pain lanced across his jaw and into his neck.

"Lay still, young master," a calm, low voice instructed him from somewhere behind him. "You'll live."

Rikard took several deep breaths to still the rising panic the pain had tindered. He slowly rolled onto his side and discovered fresh agony, twisting its way up his leg and into his hip, and he rested on his elbow for a moment, trying to master the pain.

He smelled fish and tar, and he forced one eye open to survey his world. It was still dark, but there was a faint touch of purple in the sky that heralded dawn. He was bobbing up and down, and a quick glance around showed him that he was crouched in the bottom of a small fishing boat, barely wide enough for him to stretch out his legs as he sat against the gunwale. Dark, jumbled shapes filled the bottom of the boat, and Rikard guessed at barrels and piled nets from the smell.

At the stern of the boat stood the dark shape of the fisherman. He held a long oar in his hands and steadily worked it back and forth as it propelled the boat slowly through the water.

"Where am I?" Rikard mumbled, and he gingerly ran his fingers over lips and cheek, finding swollen, bruised flesh and stinging wetness which he guessed was blood.

"Downriver from Criénne. Found you floating in the Deep Eddy, round and round to make me dizzy."

"We fell..." Rikard's voice trailed off, and he scrambled to his knees, sending the boat rocking. His hands groped frantically across the bare wood of the deck, then through the piles of gear in the prow. "Where is she?" he demanded, then he called out, "Dominique!" his voice disappearing into the gentle rush of the wide river.

"I'm sorry, young master, it was only you."

"No, she was right next to me! Go back, turn around!" Rikard pleaded.

The fisherman did not reply, but he leaned on his oar and let the current take the boat's prow until it swung to face downriver. The gentle creak of the oar began again, slow and steady and infuriating when all Rikard wanted was haste and urgency.

The eastern sky had turned a pale pink and the stars had faded by the time the boat arrived at the spot the fisherman swore he had pulled Rikard from the water. The river swung in a broad arc, wider than a bowshot, the surface serene and lazy as it slowly drifted past thick groves of trees and golden fields of wheat ripening along the shore. A small tower stood on a muddy protrusion into the river at the spot, a beacon to help pilots navigate the shallows, and a marker for the broad eddy that lurked behind it where the fisherman found his catch, and where he had discovered Rikard, slowly circling with the trapped debris of the river.

Rikard insisted that they search the backwater, leaping from the boat to peer under every bush along the shore, but it was soon apparent that Dominique was nowhere to be found.

Rikard watched the main current flow steadily past in anguish. *She could be anywhere. If this eddy didn't catch her, she might still be being dragged toward the Inner Sea, or in a dozen other eddies along the way. Or awoken at any point and swam to shore.* Rikard traced fingers across the side of his face, already swollen enough to press against his eye. *Or the fall…*

He closed his eyes and breathed away that thought.

Warm light touched his face, and he opened his eyes. A crest of brilliant gold crowned the river, and it flung a long path of sparkling and wavering light across the water that surrounded the boat. It swam and blurred as Rikard gazed at the dawn, and he angrily wiped tears away on the sleeve of his robe.

"We can go," he told the fisherman, and he slumped, miserable, against the pile of nets in the bow.

"Yes, young master," the fisherman replied, and he leaned against his oar and pushed the boat into the current once more. His steady stroke soon had the boat easing upriver, the banks slowly drifting by as the sun pulled free of the horizon behind them.

"The river is gentle all the way to the Inner Sea, young master," the fisherman tried to console him. "You could drift all day and never come to harm."

Rikard nodded, grateful for the attempt. *But, what do I do now? How do I find Dominique?* Images of a passageway filled with death tore through his mind as if enraged that they had been pushed aside in his desperation to find Dominique. *Maker, they killed Master Quentin. They killed Theirn. I can't stay in Criénne, the Garde will find me. But I can't abandon Dominique. If she's hurt, or if they find her first…*

"You must not stop until we are far from Criénne, far from Venaissin, as far from the Guild as possible." Master Quentin's voice echoed in Rikard's thoughts. *The last thing he said to us. And Dominique knows that too. She wanted to get to the docks. That's where she will go if she can. That's where I must go as well.*

Rikard pulled the Veil from his robes and idly turned it in his hand. Water ran from the cracks in its shell, and he wondered if its delicate innards had survived the dunking. *Or the fall.*

"Why do you call me young master?" Rikard asked.

"Your robes, sir," the fisherman replied, amused. "You can't live in Criénne and not know what the young masters wear."

Rikard nodded his head, dismayed. *Of course, everyone knows. Perfect.*

"Are there any boats in the docks right now?" Rikard asked. "I mean, trading ships, that might be traveling soon." Rikard winced at his bluntness. *I'm terrible at this,* he realized.

"There are, young master," the fisherman replied. "Always ships in Criénne. The docks are a busy place. Hard to avoid notice, if you don't mind my saying."

"I take your point," Rikard sighed. *Perfect, again. I have to somehow find Dominique, in the middle of a busy dock, in my apprentice robes that everyone will notice.* Rikard angrily brushed hair from his eyes and stared fiercely at the pommel of his stolen sword, wishing for a problem that could be smashed by the long steel blade. *She's gone. The river may as well have taken us to opposite sides of the Inner Sea.*

***

The fisherman had suggested, firmly, that Rikard should wade to shore some distance downriver from the city, and Rikard had quickly agreed. A short walk through the rolling pastures and cypress groves along the riverbank brought him a change of clothes, a simple brown tunic stolen from a washing line while the owner was busy with the milking. Rikard concealed his apprentice robes, the Veil, the sword, and the soggy weight that was Aldric's journal under a rock at the base of a pasture wall, and struck out feeling much less conspicuous.

But he was soon slowed to a crawl, hobbled by the throbbing pain of his swollen knee and the grinding agony of his hip, and it was long past noon by the time he limped into Criénne.

Whatever confidence he had left was shattered in the city. He did not dare do more than gaze at the docks from afar as they swarmed with soldiers of the Garde, questioning every porter, inspecting every ship, watching every sailor.

The streets around the docks were no safer. Garde patrols sent Rikard scrambling around corners at depressingly frequent intervals, and Rikard soon retreated all the way to the top of one of the hills overlooking the docks. A wide plaza crowned the hill, and Rikard rested in the shade of a tall statue, staring morosely over the red-tiled rooftops between himself and the forest of masts that marked the docks.

The steps beneath the statue were a favored spot for those who wished to praise or invile a cause, and Rikard had his choice of three speakers to listen to, although he found himself unable to care about the new taxes being levied on wheat, nor the ancestral claims to the olive groves of Roussilon, nor the supposed infidelities of Lady Cyrienne, although the last, at least, provided some amusement as the red-faced speaker tried to ignore the laughter of the crowd.

A nearby fountain provided water through the pursed lips of a dozen fat fish carved from white marble, and Rikard drank his fill and carefully washed the crusted blood from his swollen cheek until his skin blazed with stinging fire. But he could do nothing about the growling emptiness in his stomach, and he wistfully thought of the thick slices of tomato and crumbly cheese he had wolfed down at breakfast two days before, his last food of any kind.

This is useless. How can I find Dominique when I can't even get close to the docks, assuming that's where she is trying to go, as well? Assuming she came back to the city. Assuming she survived the fall. I can't even get something to eat. Do I try to steal something? Rikard had nicked pastries from a windowsill before, playing at being carefree with his friends as they idly roamed the streets of Vordoux, seeking entertainment. But they had been caught as many times as they had gotten away with it, and he did not like his chances now that capture meant much more than a stern scolding from his father and a round of mocking from his friends. *I suppose I should work for some pennies, just to buy some food, while I determine how to find Dominique. Sitting here isn't accomplishing anything.*

The first tavern he found appeared a likely candidate for employment. It had a broad terrace under a striped canvas, thick vines climbing its stone walls, and a crowd of wealthy-looking diners creating a cheerful din of voices. A shy girl perhaps a year younger than Rikard, with dark eyes and black, curly hair, was serving the patrons. "Oh! Your poor face," she gasped in sympathy, and she gave him a smile and rushed to ask her mother when Rikard inquired of whether they needed any help. The tavern owner was not as impressed with Rikard's countenance as her daughter.

"You've never cooked or cleaned in your life, have you?" she asked, glaring at his hands.

"I could scrub pots. Anything, really…"

"I don't have silver to waste on you. Nor time, so off with you."

Rikard left the tavern completely bewildered as to how he could have failed so utterly. The serving girl followed him surreptitiously, a seed loaf wrapped in a blue cloth cradled in her hands, and she quickly passed it to Rikard, whispered, "Sorry…" and raced back inside.

The remainder of his search for employment was not as successful.

A half-dozen more taverns tossed him out, often with mocking laughter, usually with curses for wasting the tavern keeper's time. When Rikard finally gave up on the dream of becoming a scullery maid and decided that a job nearer the docks made more sense, in any case, the humiliation became worse. Several of the stevedore gangs took offense at his request to join them, and he twice narrowly escaped a beating by tucking tail and limping away as fast as his leg would bear him. The nadir came when one gang offered to pay him by the crate stacked, then stood and jeered as he struggled to the point of utter exhaustion with his very first crate.

Rikard watched the evening sun paint the Guild buildings across the river bronze as he slowly nibbled his way through a sliver of the seed loaf, trying to control his urge to wolf the entire thing at once. *I have no idea how long I need to make this last.*

He had taken shelter from the Garde's dock patrols on the roof of a row of houses overlooking the river, a spot he judged to be outside the patrols' interest, but still close enough that he could easily watch the life of the docks. He had seen no sign of Dominique, which did not surprise him, as any appearance on the docks would have led to instant capture, he was sure. The merchant ships were a dead end unless he was willing to try and sneak aboard from the river and hope to conceal himself when the ship was searched, and if Dominique chose that route, he would never know.

Raised voices caught his ear, snatches of angry words floating from the docks over the constant hubbub of the city. A group of men was climbing onto the docks from one of the small boats that plied passengers back and forth across the river to the Guild, and the men were not happy. All three were dressed in fine leather vests and brightly-colored tunics, and the loudest of them was tall, with wide shoulders, thick black hair, and a trim beard. His face was dark from shouting, and his companions urged him to calm himself with raised hands and nervous glances around the docks.

"I don't care if they hear me!" the bearded man thundered, spreading his arms wide in defiance of the shining edifice on the far shore. His companions quickly surrounded him and thrust him through the doors of the nearest tavern despite his continued protests.

Rikard carefully collected the last few crumbs of his allowed portion and secured the remaining bread in its cloth, then scrambled from his perch. The tavern the three men had entered was far too close to the docks for Rikard's comfort, but he decided it was worth the risk. *Anyone that furious with the Guild might be friendly to someone the Guild is hunting,* he reasoned. *At least, it gives me a chance of help.*

Rikard skulked along the edge of the street, his face turned to the stalls of food and cheap jewelry that clustered against the buildings as he walked. Once inside the tavern, Rikard found the three men, sitting at a table near the back of the room, and snuck onto a nearby bench without meeting the tavern keeper's eye.

"... it is robbery, I agree," one of the men was saying in a hushed voice, "but how does cursing their name in the streets help?"

"What will they do?" the bearded man asked defiantly. "Double the price we already can't pay? Refuse to fix the thing we already can't afford to fix? They can choke on my cock if they think I'll mortgage my ship to them."

"What if they ban you? What if they ban your family?" the first man pointed out. "Or worse… their damn Citadelle is right across the river."

"You mean, they might ban me from buying all those Devices I can't even afford? Next, they'll be banning fish from breathing air," the bearded man scoffed, but Rikard noticed that he had lowered his voice considerably. "It's not like we're asking for a shiny Weapon. This Device helps save lives… or, at least, it did."

Rikard risked a glance toward the men. The bearded man held a small amulet with a large crystal mounted in its center. He morosely turned it back and forth to catch the light, then discarded it angrily onto the table. "Fuck the Guild," the bearded man decided.

What if it's just corroded, or has a cracked case? Rikard wondered, a vision of the bearded man tearfully thrusting a bag of silver at him shining in his thoughts. *I could fix that tonight, and maybe they would give us passage on their ship when they leave. I'd still have to find Dominique, but everything else would be taken care of.*

Rikard forced himself to stroll easily to their table. He took the remaining seat and met their surprised gazes with a brilliant smile.

"Good evening, gentlemen," Rikard greeted them. "I apologize, but I could not help overhearing your conversation."

"What do you want, boy?" the bearded man said angrily.

"I thought I could help you," Rikard assured him with a grin. "You have a Device that is broken?"

"No mystery there," one of the other men replied. "Half of Criénne knows that now."

"Is that it?" Rikard asked, pointing at the amulet on the table. Rikard could see that the Device was ancient, its silver rubbed smooth by centuries of polishing that could not hide the small dents and scratches of years of wear.

"It is," the bearded man admitted, "but it's not for sale." He tucked it into his embroidered jacket with care.

"I don't want to buy it," Rikard ruefully indicated his simple clothes. "As you can see, I am not in a position to purchase a Device. Even a broken one."

"Then what do you want?"

"I thought you might be interested in having it fixed."

"By you?"

"Yes, by me. I trained for many years in the Guild."

The bearded man's bushy eyebrows arched in astonishment, and he shared a glance with his companions before returning his gaze to Rikard.

"You're saying you were in the Guild, but now you're not."

"Correct," Rikard assured him.

The bearded man laughed softly. "You're saying you're an apostate."

The word felt like a blow to Rikard's stomach, and his grin froze on his face. *Maker's breath, he's right. I am an apostate.*

"No, I'm not." Rikard tried to meet the bearded man's stare. "I just thought I could help—"

"Yes, you are." The bearded man's gaze had turned as hard as granite. "You know what will happen to me if they find out I've even talked with you about this? I don't know you, boy."

"Whatever they do to you, it will be worse for me."

"If you are what you say you are. Listen, if you really are an apostate, then you are the stupidest one in… well, ever. Selling your services on the doorstep of the Guild itself, Martyr's tears."

"I need help, and I can help you."

"That kind of help will just bring me trouble. Now, leave us be, or I'll call the Garde, and that warning is the most kindness you'll see from me."

Rikard fled the tavern before the bubbling shame he felt roiling in his stomach could burst free, and did not stop until he had plunged into the shadows of a twisting alleyway. There, at last, he slumped against the worn stone and gave in to the pain and fear and sorrow that twisted relentlessly around his heart. Tears squeezed from his eyes as his chest shuddered to suppress a sob of despair. But he could not banish the image of blood gleaming on white cloth or the desperate fear in Theirn's wide eyes as he reached helplessly for Rikard. Nor could he banish the terrible relief that fed his shame.

Rikard wiped furiously at his eyes. *It's not good enough just to survive,* he snarled, ashamed. *Dorian took everything from us, and for what? For some thousand-year-old secret? That sailor was right. Fuck the Guild. Fuck you Dorian, and all your secrets. I'm not going to run away and hide. Not after what you've done.*

Rikard clambered shakily to his feet, his rage forcing his battered leg into motion once again.

***

Sunrise found Rikard huddled in his rooftop nest again, his jaw aching and his knee barely able to bend, exhausted from a chill night spent in pain as his mind flailed from one hopeless plan to the next.

Between the useless fantasies of revenge and the vortex of bitter recriminations, one decision had been made. Rikard crawled to the edge of the roof, unwrapped the loaf of bread, and settled in to watch for Dominique.

Rikard knew that coming to the docks was useless. There was no way aboard any of the ships, and the Garde patrols were once again examining everything that crossed the docks. But the docks were the last place that he and Dominique had tried to reach together, and that was enough to give him hope of finding her.

She will come here, just to find me, Rikard convinced himself.

He had planned to spend the day exploring the neighboring streets and rooftops, searching the places where someone watching the docks would lurk, but as he licked the last crumbs of bread from his fingers, he realized that his leg would not allow such an excursion.

Instead, he let his eyes do the exploring and settled against the stone parapet of the roof as the sun gradually banished the chill from the air and the morning mist from the river. As Rikard warmed, he gingerly examined his knee. It had turned purple overnight, swollen like a sausage with livid streaks of black and red pooling in the cracks. He could bend it slightly if he was careful, but any more movement produced flares of agony that made him dizzy.

Wonderful. Rikard sighed in frustration and turned to the river again.

A long shape was appearing from the luminous mist downriver. A sharp prow parted the placid surface of the water with barely a ripple, and a single, tall mast rose from the mist like a tower, bearing a brilliant white sail that hung limply in the still air. The ship emerged from the mist like a snake, row after row of oars slipping free from the concealing glow as the ship glided forward. Two red eyes glared from the prow, fiercely challenging any ship that dared to pass before it, and low towers graced its curved deck at both prow and stern.

The ship ignored the busy docks and headed for the Guild side of the river. Its oars danced as it spun about and slid gracefully against the piers at the base of the Guild.

Rikard watched as a swarm of sailors made the ship fast in an instant. A long column of Garde soldiers emerged from the gates and marched to the ship, their black plumes and silver armor clear even across the river. Ponderous wagons followed the soldiers, each drawn by a team of oxen who strained against their load. Rikard counted ten wagons in all, and each one took its turn slowly approaching the side of the ship.

The sailors had rigged thick cables from the arms of the mast and spent endless ages securing the cables to a network of ropes surrounding whatever was in the wagon. The sound of a capstan clicking round carried clearly to Rikard over the river, and slowly the cables took the strain. The mast bowed and the ship leaned toward the shore as a single crate rose from the wagon. The crate was far longer than it was wide or tall, perhaps twice Rikard's height, and made from a wood so dark that it appeared black.

Each of the ten wagons disgorged a similar crate, and all ten were slowly lowered into the hold of the ship. Once they were secure, the soldiers climbed aboard as well, filling the long, narrow deck.

As the wagons trundled back into the Guild, Rikard spotted a group of masters approaching the ship. At their head was Grandmaster Dorian, resplendent in his elegant robes. Dorian spoke at length with the commander of the Garde soldiers, who saluted the grandmaster and joined his men on the ship.

Defiant trumpets blared from the ship and were answered by the long bellow of the Citadelle horn. A Word pulsed from the ship, streaking the water around it as if a strong wind had suddenly whipped across its surface. The trumpets sounded again, and the banks of oars dipped in unison. The ship slipped from the pier in a long curve, rapidly picking up speed until water was thrown from its prow in two clear sheets, and it flew past Rikard's perch and disappeared downriver faster than he could have imagined.

By the time he thought to glance back at the Guild, Grandmaster Dorian was gone, and the gates were once again closed.

Rikard returned to watching the docks with renewed energy. The departure of the ship had left him feeling anxious, although he had no evidence that its mission had anything to do with him.

But his vigilance went unrewarded, and eventually he realized that he needed to descend from his perch, no matter how painful it might be, simply to seek relief for his parched mouth.

Climbing down proved to be not nearly as bad as walking, and Rikard was groaning in pain at every step by the time he reached a bubbling fountain nestled in the shadows of a marble arch. The cold water washed away the pain of his cracked lips, but he had no idea if he could make it back to his post.

This is absurd, he thought miserably as he sank to the stones next to the fountain. He closed his eyes and tried to force the throbbing agony from his leg, but thinking about it only made it worse.

Something blocked the light from the street, and Rikard blinked open his eyes and squinted at the silhouette standing over him.

"What happened to your face?" Dominique asked.

"I think my knee," Rikard replied.

Dominique knelt and grimaced as she examined his swollen knee, but all he could do was watch her. She had cut her hair, apparently by sawing it off with a knife, judging by the ragged ends, leaving it barely covering her ears. She had rubbed some kind of oil into the remaining hair, darkening it, and had clearly applied the oil to her skin as well, for it had turned from its usual rich mahogany to virtually coal black. To complete her disguise, she had dressed as a boy, in leggings and a rough vest, but that was only partially effective. Although the loose clothes concealed her shape, there was little mistaking her high cheekbones and long neck if anyone gave her more than a glance.

Still, it's more than I thought to do. All I did was smash up the side of my face.

"Come on, let's get you out of here," she said, and she helped haul him to his feet.

He tried to walk, but long before they reached his nest he was forced to lean heavily on Dominique on every step, and the slim young woman swayed under his weight. When they finally reached the house he was able to clamber up on his own, then sprawled on his back in relief once he had reached the roof.

Dominique sat next to him with her back against the parapet, and Rikard was content to watch her skin gleam in the midday sun as she breathed.

"How did you find me?" Rikard finally ventured.

"I thought you might come to the docks." Dominique opened her eyes and met his gaze. "So I've just been hiding and watching."

"Me too. I didn't know what else to do. The docks are too big."

"I saw you. Last night. There were some sailors shouting, and I saw you follow them into a tavern. At least, I thought it might be you. I wasn't sure. By the time I arrived you were gone, but the sailors were muttering about an apostate who had been in the tavern, and I guessed it must have been you."

"It was. I made a mess of trying to help them."

Dominique nodded and closed her eyes again. "At least I knew you were somewhere near, somewhere that you could see the sailors. I searched all morning until I decided that it would be easier to watch the fountains. Everyone has to drink."

"Good thinking." Rikard eased himself to join her in leaning against the parapet. "Are you all right?"

"No," she replied without opening her eyes. "I hit my head, I think, when we jumped. There's no lump, but everything seems too bright, and it makes me feel sick."

"What do we do now?"

"We do what Master Quentin said. We go far away from here, a place where the Guild will never think to search."

"That's it? We run away?"

"No. We go somewhere safe, and we watch, and we listen, and we get stronger. And when we're ready, we come back and we finish Dorian and his cronies. We burn him down."

"I like the sound of that," Rikard agreed. "Where do we go?"

"I don't know," Dominique sighed. "First, we get away from Criénne. Take a ship to somewhere far away."

"I thought about that. I don't see how we can escape on a ship. There are Garde soldiers all over the docks, and they are searching every ship."

"Of course, when the ships leave, they sail away from all that," Dominique pointed out.

***

They slipped out of Criénne that night, two shadows moving slowly east until the sun found them plodding through fields and pastures far from the city. Rikard had fashioned a branch into a crude crutch, sturdy enough to allow him to limp after Dominique across the easy terrain.

By noon they had found Rikard's hidden stash, and he gratefully pulled the sword, journal, and Device from their resting place under the stone.

They rested that night in a shepherd's hut overlooking gently rolling fields, and in the morning returned to the river and hailed a fisherman making his way downriver with one net-full of fish already flopping in the barrel secured in the middle of his small boat.

"How far are you going?" the fisherman asked as the two apprentices settled onto the nets piled in the bow of the boat.

"As far as you'll take us," Rikard replied with a wry grin. He pointed to his leg. "Every step I don't take is a blessing."

"I never did understand those that would walk when there's a river to take you," the fisherman nodded.

The fisherman pushed his boat back into the current with long sweeps of his oar, and the banks were soon slipping by in a steady flow. Willows trailed their fingers in the water, and beyond them, green pastures rolled their way into the distance, dotted with the distant shapes of cows languidly questing for daffodils amongst the grass.

"Do you ever see any large ships on the river?" Rikard asked. "Ones that might be going a bit farther?"

Dominique rolled her eyes at his bluntness, but he just shrugged. *I'll never be good at this, and the fisherman doesn't care, so why not ask?*

"One that might be going to the Inner Sea?" the fisherman asked. "Or farther, are you thinking?"

"Farther," Rikard replied.

"I do, most every day," the fisherman told them. "Like this fine ship, for example. She looks ready to sail wherever the winds can take her."

Rikard glanced up, wondering if the fisherman meant the tiny boat they traveled in. But the fisherman smiled and pointed upriver, and Rikard twisted to follow his finger. Tall masts stood above the trees that covered a bend in the river, carrying brown sails that appeared to float above the tree tops like rogue clouds. As Rikard watched, the ship rounded the bend. She had bulging sides that curved out of the water and a wide deck that swooped from a bluff bow to a high stern. Two great masts rose from the deck, with enough spars that they resembled a forest in winter, but only the tops carried sails as the ship rode the slow current downstream, just enough to provide steerage as she stuck diligently to the central channel.

Rikard saw that the ship sat extremely low in the water, but even so, her sides towered above him as the fisherman guided his boat alongside. Hails were exchanged, and the fisherman tucked his boat under the ship's rail and caught a flung line, and they were quickly in tow. Rikard grabbed at the sides as the boat tilted alarmingly, but the fisherman appeared unconcerned, exchanging pleasantries with the crew peering over the rail at them.

"Do you have fish to sell?" a bearded face with ruddy cheeks and a wide-brimmed hat yelled down, although his accent was so thick that it took a moment for Rikard to realize that the sailor was speaking Common. Rikard's Common was not good at the best of times, and he could not remember the last time he had used it. *Before I left for the Guild, at any rate. I hope someone up there speaks Venaissine.*

"A half a barrel, caught just this morning. And these young gentlemen here might want a word with the captain if it pleases."

"That would be me," the bearded face replied, and Rikard groaned inwardly.

"Good morning," Rikard squeezed some Common from the far recesses of his tired brain. "My name is Rikard. Where does you go?"

"Home to Albyn, with a full hold, thank the Maker."

"Albyn?" The name was familiar, but for a moment Rikard could not recall from where. Then with a flash he remembered. *The Marquessa's sister, Gabrielle… that's where she went when she married. She's the Queen of Albyn, or something like that.*

"Yes, Albyn. Greymouth, really, although we have some goods for Bandirma to land on the way."

Rikard was hardly listening, so difficult was the Captain's accent, but that caught his attention, and Quentin's voice echoed in his thoughts as if the master was sitting on the piled nets next to him. *"I can send a message to their Archivist in Bandirma, a man named Whitebrooke…"*

"You are go to Bandirma? The Temple place?"

"That's right. One hundred casks of plonk for the Temple, and seven crates of the finest for some of the taverns in town."

A place far from the Guild, where they will never search, and the place that Quentin thought we might find out more about Duibhir.

"Can you take us, please?"

"I don't need any crew if that's what you're thinking. Not a lad with no experience, straight from the scriptorium by the look of you, beg your pardon."

Rikard frowned. He had not thought of working his way to Albyn, but he realized that they were not about to get invited along for the ride out of good will, which had been his first plan.

"Perhaps we are a passenger?"

"Can you pay, lad?" The captain ran a skeptical eye over Rikard and Dominique, and then frowned and gave her a second long, appraising, glance.

"This sword is very nice. You may have it."

"Hop up and let's see it, then."

A ladder was lowered to the boat, and Rikard clung to it while he was shoved and pulled over the rail amidst a chorus of laughter and good-natured advice. Dominique followed much more gracefully as he disentangled himself from the sword belt and offered it to the captain.

The seaman slipped the blade free and examined the light reflecting from its steel with a practiced eye.

"Very nice work. Very nice." The captain returned the blade to its sheath with a snap. "This is your sword, you say?"

"It is *your* sword," Rikard corrected, "if you take us to Bandirma."

The captain pondered his decision for far longer than Rikard thought possible, leaving the apprentice squirming with worry. Then a smile burst through the shaggy beard and he clapped Rikard on the shoulder.

"You've had a hard-enough time, by the looks of it. It's a deal then."

Rikard nodded gratefully and waved to the fisherman as his boat dropped astern, watching him slowly stroke his oar back and forth as his little boat disappeared around a bend. Then Rikard left the rail and was introduced to the berth that was to be their home on the voyage north. It was small and was to be shared with two of the ship's mates.

"They snore a bit, but they'll not bother you, lass," the captain said to Dominique. "They know they'll be swimming home if they do."

Dominique nodded and smiled, although Rikard had to translate the captain's words once he had left.

"This is how it was on my voyage to Criénne." She shrugged, unconcerned. "Better, since we have a door, this time. Look, they have hammocks for us. I had forgotten how peaceful it is to sleep in a hammock."

With Dominique's help, Rikard crawled into a hammock and lost himself in the gentle creak of the ship, suddenly exhausted with the relief that there were thick wooden walls and growing distance between him and the searching eyes of the Garde.

THE END

Book One of
The Chronicles of the Martyr

The Martyr's Blade

***

When a series of gruesome rituals are discovered in the icy hinterlands of Albyn, three of the realm's most storied guardians are sent to track down and bring those responsible to justice.

Lord Bradon, veteran commander and warrior, driven by his unabating love for a woman forever beyond his reach. Sir Killock, a Templar knight more at home in the endless wilderness than in any castle or court. The paragon Danielle d'Lavandou, heir to the Martyr's Blade, a legendary weapon guarded by her ancestors for generations.

What they uncover is far more than simple murder: a terrifying threat to all the realms of mankind, thought sealed away so long ago that it now exists only as legend.

Available Now

Tales From the Martyr's World

The Thief's Tale

A Novel

***

When an audacious burglary goes spectacularly right, Wyn expects her young life to change for the better. Glorious infamy and the respect and adulation of her underworld brethren will, at least, buy her a few drinks, and just might convince the other thieving vermin to keep their knives to themselves for a while.

But when her new-found reputation attracts the worst kind of attention, she is forced to take on an impossible heist, working for a vicious killer named Quinn, a man she has feared and hated since she was an orphan fighting for food on the streets.

Faced with the destruction of everything that holds meaning to her, Wyn vows to pull the greatest job of all, to beat Quinn at his own brutal game.

Available Soon

About the Author

Joel Manners has created rich worlds and memorable characters in video games for more than 30 years. He brings his talent for storytelling to the epic fantasy genre in his critically acclaimed series, *The Chronicles of the Martyr.* He lives in Austin, TX with his wife and two boys. And this dog his wife made them get, but honestly, she's pretty sweet. The dog. His wife too. Although he suspects that might change if she sees this.

Made in the USA
Coppell, TX
21 December 2019

13569484R00065